RUBY RISING

RUBY RISING

JOHN H. MATTHEWS

BLUEBULLSEYE PRESS

RUBY RISING
Written by John H. Matthews
©2023 John H. Matthews

ISBN: 978-1-970071-12-2

Library of Congress Control Number: 2023920914

Bluebullseye Press
A division of Bluebullseye LLC

Edited by Shea Megale

Cover design ©2023 John H. Matthews

Also by John H. Matthews

Designated Survivor
Family Line
The More a Thing is Perfect

The Eddie Holland Detective Series:
The South Coast
Ballyvaughan
Hang Fire

Children's Books (Middle Grade):
Runt

For my boy, Brennan.

Watching you grow up is the

greatest joy in my life.

PROLOGUE

Buster Ballard took a quick step toward the fire to avoid another attack from the small man in the black hoodie. Long, dancing shadows of their arms and legs mimicked them on the ground as they fought. He felt the heat searing him in only his dirty jeans, the fire reflecting off his bare sooty skin.

The smell of burning tires, melting beer cans, and whatever else had been thrown onto the pile the last week filled the air. It was heavy and hard to breathe. Buster felt it cake the inside of his nostrils while inhaling heavily in his fight to live.

As a fist struck him across the face again, Buster recalled the moment before the fight where he thought he could win. It wasn't his first fight, and had won more than he'd lost. But this was different. This opponent was different. The man he faced now had experience and skills beyond anything Buster had seen before. It was beyond someone who trained in a downtown boxing gym. The man was a professional and blended fighting arts from all over the world into a fury of clean, smooth attacks.

Buster tried to keep up, to minimize the impacts of the short strikes that hurt as if each were from a Louisville slugger. When he finally landed a punch on the man's head, he heard the cheers around him, but they were a blur. He couldn't take the slightest bit of a second to turn to them or even acknowledge them, because the next barrage of punches and kicks from the small man would follow and he knew he had to be ready to defend himself, to try to get another strike in. To try to survive.

A combination attack of punches and kicks spun toward him with no way to anticipate what would come next. Buster stepped back without a single hit landing on him, though he knew the hooded man could have connected with each one and ended the fight. But the men surrounding them wanted more. The man who stood surrounded by bodyguards wanted more.

He's playing with me, Buster thought. *He's fucking playing with me.*

He accepted his time was too short to do anything, to have a chance at coming out alive. He had seen the small foreign man defeat others easily, then watched as their bodies, limp and barely alive, were thrown into the back of a pickup truck to be unceremoniously dropped off near the hospital twenty miles away. No word ever came back if the men lived or died. Once you left camp, you were forgotten and replaced.

A kick to his chest sent Buster falling backward, scrambling with his feet to find purchase in the soil, arms swinging in the air to keep from falling into the fire that now grew taller, a living thing threatening anything that came close. Flames arced and spun. Occasionally there were loud bangs, then pieces of red hot shrapnel struck his skin from the spray cans the other men would throw into the fire to distract them. Once, a few months ago, a piece hit a fighter in the eye. The small hooded man never slowed his attack even as the fighter doubled over in pain, clawing at his face. Buster saw him after. A shard of a WD-40 can had sliced the eyeball and cauterized it at the same time, leaving it protruding with burned skin holding the metal in place.

Another small explosion from the fire and the hooded man stopped as he came toward Buster with a series of kicks. He pawed at his hoodie where a piece of metal struck him. It had cut through the cotton and burned his arm. The small man pulled the jacket off over his head. It was the first time Buster, or any of the onlookers, had seen him without it no matter how hot it was in the Texas desert.

The man had long black hair that had been pulled back but now flew loose around his head, the band that held it together coming off with the hoodie. He wore a black long sleeve and skin tight dry fit shirt and black pants but looked more like a homeless man or a weird uncle than the warrior he was. Without the hood, Buster could see the man's eyes glow green in the fire. He was older than any of them thought he was. Late forties at least. Perhaps more. Nobody knew his name. They just called him the hooded man. Rumors went around that he'd been a soldier in Nepal. Another said he had been an assassin. Either was believable.

Buster was only twenty-four years old and physically in his prime, but malnourished from what little food made it to the camp. Like the rest of the men, he worked hard to be noticed, to be promoted and moved to the ranch where he would eat and drink well. He craved only to belong somewhere for the first time in his life, to be accepted, to be in service to the Ruby.

Seconds dragged out as if in slow motion. If he could beat this man, he would surely be taken to the ranch. He went there once before his initiation. The gleaming white farm house had a red roof and a porch where he'd seen the Ruby sitting and speaking with the Second. It made him feel closer to the Ruby. The Second lived only one building over from Buster at the compound down the road and they spoke often. Perhaps he would put a word in for him, if he could gain favor.

Buster sidestepped the small man's next attack and landed his second strike of the fight, a left hook against the side of his head. He thought there was a stagger, a momentary loss of balance, and moved in again. Another punch to the head while the Nepali was still shaken. A kick into his gut which landed solid as if against a tree rather than flesh and bones. His leg retracted, then swung out again only higher, landing in the man's face. He swore he felt the crunch of cartilage against his shin. As his leg dropped, though, the small man was smiling at him, a trickle of blood running down from his nose.

It was the last strikes Buster would land on his opponent.

The yelling of the men around him merged with the roaring of the fire. It was a guttural, primal sound that frightened Buster while at the same time encouraged him. He was part of that audience several times, and knew that the cheering wasn't as much for the fighter but for the fight. They wanted blood. He stepped in with a right that missed its target as the small man took a stutter step and landed three blows to Buster's head. He didn't feel the impacts, but heard the coinciding cracks inside his skull. Blackness crept in slowly from the edges of his vision. He had suffered a concussion once in a junior high football game and this felt the same, but worse.

The roaring and yelling was gone. There was only silence, but for a high-pitched tone that grew louder with each passing second. He stood, arms to his side with no instinct left to raise them. His mind still planned the next moves, the next strikes, the next defense, but his body was unwilling to accept any commands.

He saw the small man before him. His skin alternated between light brown and orange as the fire beside them fluctuated and spiraled. The man's green eyes didn't move off him as Buster waited for the next strike that he knew would end him, or at least end his time in the service of the Ruby.

But that hit didn't come. The small man lowered his arms and looked at Buster, and he thought he saw the faintest nod, the smallest sign of respect to another warrior.

Buster was already unconscious when his knees gave way. His body buckled and fell into the flames, drawn by the magnetic pull of the fire. The smell of his burning flesh mixed with the acrid scent of the melting tires. Two men ran over and pulled him away by his legs.

Another would take his place in the group of twelve, as he had taken another man's who fell to the Nepali.

CHAPTER 1

The sun reflects off the water and sand, forcing me into an eternal state of squinting. Even with my sunglasses on I'm resigned to seeing everything through slits to avoid blindness. It's not even noon and I'm melting in the heat. And what is that smell? Rotten fish? Old fast food? Patchouli covered college kids? All of them combined? I've never been a beach person, except for running beside it.

I act as though I'm enjoying myself, of course. Anything less will be met with a continual stream of *"what's wrong?"* and that is no way to spend a vacation.

Eva is stunning in her two-piece beside me. She is face down on her towel, the strap to her top untied to avoid tan lines. I enjoy looking at her perfectly smooth skin. So that's one thing I like about the beach.

"Hey, look at that!" I say.

"Stop it, Eddie."

"What?"

"I'm not going to sit up quickly so you can see my boobs," she says. "And you see them all the time, so I don't know why you keep trying that."

"Because I like to see them."

"Stop it."

"Please?"

She groans loudly, raises her head, and looks around. I'm sitting on my low folding beach chair beside her. I hate sitting on the sand, even on a towel. Sand just gets everywhere it shouldn't be. Eva rolls slightly onto her side, exposing her breasts to me, then is back down, face into the hole formed by her crossed arms.

"Yeah. Boobies."

"You are such a child."

"I'm fine with that."

"Sadly, so am I."

It is the final morning of a quick three-day trip to Padre Island as partial make up for having to cancel our real vacation a few months ago due to a case. She hasn't let me forget it, so I booked a condo on the beach and we drove down Friday morning.

"Mmmm . . . I don't want to go home." Her voice is muffled in the crook of her arms.

I look around at the garbage in the sand and take a whiff of the ocean air again. Dirty feet? Dead seagulls?

"Yeah. Me either."

"What time is it?"

I look at my phone, which was easy since I've been staring

at it all morning, except for the momentary appearance of boobs. "Eleven-fifteen."

She sighs. "Guess we'd better go clean up and hit the road."

With our beach gear folded up and packed into a tote bag the size of which I've never seen, we walk back up the sand to the porch of our condo. She rinses off in the outside shower first then goes in for a proper wash. I stand with the cold water flowing down over me for a long while, knowing I have plenty of time before my turn in the bathroom. I look out over the shining sand and sparkling water. I guess it isn't that bad. Except for the smell.

As much as I complain to myself, I would go anywhere with her, for her. A dirty beach. The Great Pacific Garbage Patch. Florida. Just being with her is my vacation from everything else.

My phone chimes as I walk inside. A text from Gus. My oldest friend, he runs the Austin office of the FBI. Since taking an indefinite leave of absence from the bureau, I do work for him in order to gain access to their systems for my private detective clients. In the long run I end up doing far more for them than I do for me.

Call me. DB in Salt Creek. Can you go?

I call him.

Gus answers on the first ring. "Are you headed back from the beach yet?"

"Getting ready to go in somewhere between five minutes and an hour."

"I understand."

"What's so urgent?"

"I need someone to get out to Salt Creek to check out a dead body at the hospital there."

"I have so many questions. Am I just someone now? Where the hell is Salt Creek? Why are you checking out a dead body? Did Hope break up with you?"

"What? No. We got a call on the tip line from a nurse. They had a man come in last night unconscious who didn't make it to morning. She said his wounds were . . . unique."

"What do you mean unique?"

"She's seen them before on other patients."

"Then they're not unique, are they?"

"Okay, okay, they are like each other but not like any others? I don't know. I talked to her briefly but she wasn't comfortable discussing it on the phone."

"Why did she call the FBI? Shouldn't this be local or state jurisdiction?"

"There is no local PD, and she said there were markings on his body that she thought would be more along our lines."

"Markings?"

"Tattoos."

"Of?"

"Swastikas and shit."

"Oh, great. White supremacists are always fun to deal with."

"I said I'd get someone out there today, but I'm stretched thin with other cases and agents out on vacation."

I exhale loudly enough for him to hear to show my false annoyance. "Sure."

"Will Eva be okay with this?"

"No."

"Thanks, Eddie."

"Text me the details."

CHAPTER 2

"Of course I don't mind, sweetie," Eva says. "There's nothing I love more on my vacation from the hospital where I see dead bodies than going to a different hospital to see a dead body."

I feel the full force of her sarcasm like a dump truck running over my body, then backing up and running over me again. Repeatedly.

"I'm sorry."

She smiles. "Really, it's fine. More time with you before we go back to the real world in the morning."

I drive in quiet contemplation of the woman beside me. Her long, bare legs are crossed in the tiny passenger seat area of her Fiat 500 and she looks the Italian part with her wide brimmed white beach hat still on because she didn't dry her hair before we left. I can't tell the difference. She still looks amazing. Dry hair. Wet hair. The years since I met her are the best of my life, with no hyperbole. She makes me a better person and I like to think I make her a better person, but she was damn near perfect when we met.

There is an unknown that hangs between us, though. I very publicly asked her to marry me some time ago, but we have yet to discuss any plans. There isn't a tension over it, just a silence. I haven't seen any copies of *Modern Bride* magazine in the house or missed any subtle hints to faraway destinations for a honeymoon. I don't *think* I've missed any, at least. I like to think I"m a pretty good detective, so it would be embarrassing if I have. We live together, laugh a lot, drink wine and beer and eat good food. On mornings after a late shift we make love with the sun coming through the sheer curtains on the high windows in the bedroom, then shower together. Things are good.

The town of Salt Creek sits out in the Texas plains a few hours west of Austin. On the map I see no sign of a creek so the name of the town must be ironic. Even without the navigation on my phone, we could have found the hospital within a few minutes of driving around. It is a low, one-story affair in a shade of brown that blends in with the dead grass and bare soil surrounding it. A large H is painted on the small parking lot for helicopters to land. I imagine the calls over the intercom for employees and visitors to move their vehicles while a medical chopper hovers overhead, waiting on rusty F-150s and Silverados to get out of the way.

We enter through the the emergency room doors to a four-bed area. It is very quiet, even for a Sunday afternoon.

All of the beds are empty and nobody is in sight.

"I'd love for my E.R. to be this quiet just once," Eva says.

"Can I help you?"

We jump at the voice, then see the brown hair barely level with the high registration desk, plexiglass running from the counter up to the ceiling with a round hole cut in it to allow people to speak. The woman is looking down at an open book on the desk.

"Hi, yes. I'm looking for Rebecca Morgan."

Without moving her head, she picks up the telephone and presses a button. Her voice comes over the intercom. "Becks, you have visitors at emergency." The phone is set back on the cradle.

"Thank you," I say.

There's another click and shuffling sound over the speakers broadcasting throughout the hospital a woman's voice who is obviously chewing something.

"Is it T.J.?"

The woman at the counter picks the phone up again.

"No." She finally looks up at us. "Nobody from around here."

The conversation continues for all to hear.

"All right, Sheila. Can ya send 'em down to the cafeteria?"

I look at Eva. She is smiling. I recognize the smile. It is her "Am I in an alternate universe?" smile. That smile is directed at me quite often.

After some very simple directions, we walk through a pair of swinging doors out of the emergency room and onto the main hospital floor. All of the room doors are are propped open and televisions blare from a few of them.

The cafeteria is a small room at the end of that same hallway. Food service consists of three vending machines and an old white refrigerator with *NURSES ONLY* in black magic marker written on the door. Not on a piece of paper taped to the door, but right on the door. One woman is sitting at a table staring up at a television. I would say it is NASCAR or a rodeo playing on it, but I don't really look to see.

"Rebecca Morgan?" I say.

"Yeah." She mutes the television with a remote and turns to look at us, a sandwich in her hand. "You don't look like FBI agents."

"We won't take that personally," I say. She didn't invite us to call her Becks. I do take that personally.

"I'm Eddie Holland. I work for the FBI out of the Austin office. This is my partner, Dr. Eva Taylor. I mean, like, my girlfriend partner. My partner in life. Not my FBI partner."

Eva is staring at me as if I have something wrong with my brain.

"Okay," Rebecca says, looking at us both as if we have something wrong with our brains. "I talked to that Mexican FBI guy on the phone."

"Yes." I nod slowly, absorbing her statement while standing next to my obviously Latina fiancée. "He told me you had a dead body that raised some suspicion."

"Only with me. The other nurses think I'm crazy," Rebecca says. "He was dumped down by the turn to the hospital. Luckily someone driving by saw him and called us."

"They called you? They didn't come down to the E.R. to tell you, or help get the injured person here?"

"No. They just called. The four of us on duty took a stretcher down to the street and he was in bad shape. He was unconscious and beaten up really bad. When we got him back into the light he was even worse than we thought. One arm and the side of his face were burned. His body was bruised all up and down. That's when I saw his tattoos."

"Special Agent Ramirez said you've seen injuries like this before?"

"I have. One a few months ago, another a while before that."

"They both die?"

"No. Not while here, at least. No idea what else they got themselves into after leaving, but they both walked out on their own."

"Can we see the body?"

"You seen a dead body before?"

"Well, FBI agent and doctor." I point at myself then Eva. "So, yeah. A few times."

"It's your party." The nurse packs up the rest of her lunch into a Teen Titans padded lunchbox.

"You have kids?" Eva says.

"No."

It is on the way to the morgue we find out that the hospital has another hallway, doubling the number of hallways I previously thought it had. Nurse Rebecca slides the ID card that hangs around her neck on a neon pink springy elastic cord across a black sensor and the door unlocks. Inside, she hands us both masks from a cardboard box.

"We're waiting for someone from the state to come get him. We don't have facilities here to take care of it."

There are only four cooler drawers for bodies. She opens the first one and slides it out. A white blanket covers the body.

"I've seen this one enough. I'm gonna trust that the two of you aren't here to do any weird shit, so you can find me back in emergency when you're done."

"Nope. No weird shit here," I say.

"Mmhmm." Nurse Rebecca leaves and the heavy door slams shut.

I turn to Eva. "Is weird shit in morgues common?"

"More than you'd think."

"Gross."

I uncover the body down to his waist. The skin tone is pale from death but the bruises are still dark, deep shades of purples and greens. His right arm has second degree burns, as well as the right side of his face.

He was fit, when he was alive, at least. Even in death he has good definition to his muscles and traces of six-pack abs. The first of several swastika tattoos is in the center of his chest, maybe eight inches across. A bold statement during swimsuit season, for sure. Another smaller one is on his right upper arm with writing in what I think is supposed to be German around it. My favorite, though, is across his stomach where it says AREAN NATION.

"Someone needed spell check," I say to no reaction.

"The wounds are consistent with a fight," Eva says. "His knuckles are bruised and cut, and the patterns across his chest and abdomen look like they're from very strong punches and kicks."

Eva grabs a pair of rubber gloves from a box on the wall

and pulls them on more easily than I've ever seen it done.

"You've seen this kind of bruising before?" I say.

"You mean, other than on you on multiple occasions?"

"Touché."

"None of the visible wounds would account for death. Even the burns."

She is in full on doctor mode and I stand back and watch her work. It is something I don't get to see, except for the many times she's had to treat me.

"Here." She points at his head. "You see the bruising behind the ears? That's called Battle's sign."

"You mean like— "

"No," she interrupts before I can finish. "It has nothing to do with being in a battle. It's named after a British surgeon, Dr. William Henry Battle."

"Well, that's unnecessarily confusing."

"True, especially given that Battle's sign only shows up after severe trauma. It shows that at least one bone in the skull is broken." She palpates his skull, running her fingers along his head. "I'd say at least two or more. Especially on this side. I would bet he took a very hard direct hit here."

"Could that kill him?"

"Impossible to say without an autopsy, but it could." She puts two fingers on the side of his head, just above his ear and pushes. "See that movement? If the impact was hard enough, it could puncture the three layers of the meninges. This could cause you to bleed out internally. Or the hit could have severed the brain stem."

"Pretty safe to say that his deadness is directly related to having been in a fight, then."

"In my professional opinion," she looks back down at the body. "Maybe."

She pulls the rubber gloves off and drops them in a trash can.

"So, what kind of gross shit do people do in morgues?"

"You really don't want to know."

CHAPTER 3

Shirtless, sweaty, and running across the bridge with downtown Austin behind me, I make the turn into Zilker Park. I love the house we share a few miles east, but miss running in the city.

She always says I only listen to albums that are twenty years old, so I have *Remember That You Will Die* by Polyphia streaming from my watch to wireless earbuds. I miss when I didn't even have a cellphone, but damn is this handy.

I moved back to Austin to get away from the FBI, D.C., and the constant stress and workload. After nearly fifteen years in counterterrorism, I was broken and needed a rest and change of scenery. Since moving back, I've had two cars destroyed and have been in the emergency room so many times I should get a frequent flyer card. Somehow, this is still less stress than being at the Washington Field Office going over stacks of intel from Middle East sources. I began working for the bureau again as an independent contractor of sorts a few years ago and it is the best of both worlds.

And of course I met Eva here. That kinda outweighs any of the bad things that have happened.

I slow to a walk, arms raised, hands on my head to catch my breath as I come back down the sidewalk to Buddy's Music Saloon. The bar had been an unplanned addition in my life two years ago when I watched Buddy, a high school friend of mine, killed on the floor of his own club due to a case I was working. The family didn't want the place, so Gus went in as a silent partner and we bought it. The almost nightly live music keeps customers coming in and buying beer, so it covers its own costs most of the time.

It's several hours until my bar manager shows up to prepare for tonight's show. I'm tempted to pull a beer from the draught, but decide not to. I check my phone and a number I don't recognize is in the missed calls. No voicemail. I tap to dial the number. A woman answers.

"Hello?"

"Hi. This is Eddie Holland. I had a missed call from this number."

"Oh, yeah. I didn't know what to do, if I should leave a message or not."

"We're talking now so you don't have to worry about it."

"Right. True. So I got a name on that dead man for you. State police finally got him identified."

I finally realize it's the nurse, Rebecca Morgan. Guess we're friendly enough now she doesn't have to say her name, even though it's been two weeks since I met her. I consider calling her Becks but still don't know if I'm allowed.

"Really. That's great. Not for the dead guy, I guess, but you know what I mean."

Silence on the other end of the line.

"So, what's his name?"

"Ballard. Buster Ballard."

"Buster? Is that a name people really give their children?"

"I have two nephews named Buster."

"I guess it is, then."

She gives me the address they got for Buster Ballard and we hang up. I text the information to Gus.

In the back room, I change out of my running shorts into cargo shorts, liberally spread some deodorant in my pits, and pull on my old At the Drive-In concert T-shirt from the 2000 tour for their *Relationship of Command* album. I can't recall the last time I wore a shirt with a collar. Or a shirt that wasn't from a concert, for that matter.

Gus's office is north of downtown and I pick up a pineapple, beet, and jalapeño smoothie from a shop on Brazos Street on my way. I know Gus will not be offended that I didn't get him one.

I buzz into the building with my badge and make my way to his office. Men in dark suits and women in conservative blouses and slacks look busy as I slurp my smoothie. I find Gus sitting behind his desk staring at paperwork.

"And this is why I don't miss being an agent anymore," I say. "The paperwork killed me."

"If you do it immediately and not procrastinate until the last minute, it isn't that bad."

"How much of each day is spent filling out reports?"

"Most of it."

"I rest my case."

"What was that text about?" Gus says. "And what on earth are you drinking? Is that a even a natural color?"

"Very natural, and supposedly very healthy. I'll be pooping for a week after this."

"Good to know."

"The nurse from Salt Creek a couple weeks ago." I suck out the last of the blended fruits and get a chunk of jalapeño. "She called me with the name and address of the dead guy you had me and Eva check out."

"Figured it was something to do with that. I have Malone pulling info, and I checked the address out on satellite imagery."

"Satellite imagery?"

He shrugs. "Yeah."

"Do you mean Google Maps?"

"It works, okay?"

"If you like three year old images."

"I can't call and just get current aerial shots whenever I want."

"I'm not judging."

"You are."

"A little. So what did you find on Google Maps?"

"The . . . satellite imagery . . . shows a group of small houses and a trailer about twenty miles east of Salt Creek. It's off a farm road and fairly secluded."

"You pick up any heat signatures on your satellite imagery? Any life forms? WMD's?"

"Shut up."

Special Agent Malone steps into the office and hands Gus a file.

Gus flips through the pages. I'm not the greenest earth-hugging person there is, but I shake my head at the thought of everything getting printed out and put into its own jacket to either be filed away and eventually end up in the warehouse from the end of *Raiders of the Lost Ark,* or to be shredded unceremoniously.

"What did Malone find in his Google search of Buster Ballard? Did he have a MySpace page detailing his criminal activities? What song played when he opened the page? Let me guess. "Hit me Baby One More Time" by Britney Spears? "Eye of the Tiger" by Survivor?"

Gus glares at me over the top of the paper.

"Buster Oliver Ballard. Twenty-four years old. Born in El Paso. Served nine months for assault and battery, and possession of an illegal firearm."

"Sounds like an exciting guy. And his real name is Buster?" I shake my head. "Who'd have thought. What was his last known address before Salt Creek?"

"Lockup. Looks like he was released and unaccounted for a few months before landing in Salt Creek."

"From jail to hell," I say.

Gus looks back at the map on the screen. "Sure doesn't look like a luxury resort."

"Where does this leave us?" I lean back in my chair and shoot a two-pointer with my smoothie cup into the grey plastic trash can beside the desk. "Is there anything actionable to follow up on or is it case closed on old Buster?"

"Something doesn't smell right," he says.

"That's probably the smoothie. It's an acquired taste."

"That's for sure, but with Buster."

"Shouldn't we just hand it over to state police or the Rangers?"

"It'll get cold cased and filed away faster than that smoothie is going to go through you with either of them." Gus turns his chair to stare at the wall. It's how he thinks things over. No distractions. "Swastikas and white supremacist tattoos. Arrested for illegal firearms. Goes from right out of lockup to a compound in the middle of the Texas plains."

"I think I know where you're going with this," I say.

"Militia."

"Yoga retreat. I mean, what you said."

"Wanna go on a road trip?"

"Back to Salt Creek, or somewhere nice?"

Another glare as he stands up. "And it's just "Baby One More Time." There's no 'hit me.'"

CHAPTER 4

I get into the black Ford Explorer that stops at the curb outside the home I share with Eva. It was really her home first, before we met, but I've adopted it. Or it's adopted me. Can a house adopt you? I moved in, let's put it that way.

Gus is in jeans and a black T-shirt.

"Is this FBI casual chic?" I say.

"It's *I haven't done laundry in a week* chic." Gus pulls away from the curb. "When are you going to get a new car, anyway? Would be nice not to keep racking up miles on my company vehicle. You could expense the miles, you know."

"And use valuable taxpayer money?"

"What do you think we're doing with this thing?"

"True. But you enjoy driving it."

"I do."

"I need to get something. Eva says she doesn't mind me using her Fiat, but I know she'd rather I get my own car."

"We get some fleet cars that age out. I'm sure you could pick up one of those on the cheap."

"Thanks, but no thanks. I'd rather not roll around in an eight-year-old Chevy Malibu with AM radio and a big antenna bolted to the trunk. Anyway, you know me. I like older cars."

"I'll keep my eyes open for junkers for sale."

"Thanks. Did you bring enough water for us both?" I look in the backseat.

"I did."

"Did you check to see how many Sonics there are between here and there?"

"Three."

"Excellent."

I connect my phone to the USB cable I keep in his glovebox for such occasions, since he never has any music in the SUV. He listens to podcasts and horrible things like that.

"What's it going to be?" Gus says. "The same Guy Clark album we've listened to for twenty years? Lyle Lovett again? Spoon for the billionth time?"

"If you want, I have a playlist with all of the above."

"No. Just, something different."

I hit play on my phone and sit back as the opening riffs of "This Land" by Gary Clark, Jr. come through the less than adequate base model speakers of the Ford Explorer.

"This will get us about a third of the way there," I say. "And tell you what, I'll let you choose the second album."

"There's this great podcast about— "

"No."

"It's my car."

"Whatever."

We've been friends since we were young. Junior high at least. Maybe before. He's just always been there for me, and me for him. The only time we spent in different cities was after we got our assignments out of Quantico. He was sent to the Midwest to begin his slow climb, and since 9/11 had just happened and I'd shown interest in counterterrorism, I was sent to Washington, D.C. where I drove a desk for several years. There were occasions to get into the field, but instead of sitting in a fake flower delivery van outside a suspected mobster's house in Chicago, I was working with the Joint Terrorism Task Force and flying through Afghanistan in C-130 cargo planes with Army Rangers and Navy SEALs. They did the jumping and shooting. I provided the intel.

Gus found his way back to the Austin satellite office and took over a few years ago. I took a leave of absence from the bureau and came home, only to find myself contracting back to the FBI, still carrying my creds and weapon almost everywhere I go.

The plains west of Austin have no movement to them. Slight rises and falls in the landscape but nothing dynamic. It isn't like the deserts of Utah or New Mexico. You easily find yourself staring at a point in the distance while driving just to find you are about to go off the highway. It's numbing, but in a way soothing at the same time.

The navigation screen is showing our destination after a right turn onto a dirt road. We both watch out the window as we pass it. He takes the next turn a half mile down then cuts through the field. There's no fences since there doesn't seem to be anything to keep in or out. There isn't much in the way of farmland or livestock out here. The usual crop of West Texas is plentiful, the big steel pump jacks that siphon crude oil out of the earth and into a network of pipelines that run underground in some places, and right across the plains in others. The area is at the eastern edge of the Permian Basin, which produces 20% of the nation's crude. You would think the area would benefit from the oil, but the people making the money off it live far away from the desolate plains. Once the pipelines are built, they need little maintenance. A few people per region watch and fix them as needed.

Gus stops the SUV at the edge of a slightly elevated area. The address we're looking for is half a mile away. We both grab binoculars.

"Can't see much from here," I say.

"Nope."

"Get much closer and they'll see us, though." The sun will reflect off the car and be visible for miles.

"Yup."

"What's a boy to do?"

"We could walk."

I look around. "Isn't it like 200 degrees out there?"

Gus looks at the temperature displayed on his dashboard. "106."

"Like I said."

"But it's a dry heat."

We get out and grab the small go bags we keep in his

SUV and load each with six bottles of water, the binoculars, and a few energy bars. I see he has his Sig Sauer P229 on his hip. I have my Glock 17 with two extra magazines. He has a pair of tan floppy hats with venting and wicking and all kinds of stuff designed to keep your head cool. They work for about two minutes then are soaked through with sweat.

It's an easy walk, as walks go. As long as you watch the ground to keep from tripping over scrub brush. Gus is ten feet ahead of me and after a while comes to a stop, his fist rising in the air beside his head instinctively to communicate to me not to move.

He takes several slow steps backwards, then turns left and makes a wide circle.

"Rattlesnake," he says.

"Well this just got more fun."

So now the walk is easy as long as you keep from tripping on scrub brush or stepping on a deadly venomous snake.

We reach the next low rise and check the ground around us for rattlesnakes before getting on our bellies. The compound is a couple hundred yards away now. The binoculars do a much better job of giving us a view of the area than they did at half a mile.

"There's a fence surrounding the compound," Gus says. "Didn't see that on the satellite images."

"You talking about Google Maps again?"

"Yes. Google Maps."

"Sometimes those images are several years old, especially in lower population areas," I say. "So the fence could easily have been built in the last few years or even months."

"Looks like maybe some old oil field shacks. One sliding

gate in the fence." Gus adjusts his body in the dirt to better prop the binoculars against his face. "What do we have here?"

"Where?"

"Southeast corner. Two men with assault rifles."

"Sentries?"

"If they are, they're not too good at their jobs. They're just standing there smoking."

"Probably just a peaceful camp full of friendly armed militia," I say.

"Right."

We identify at least ten different men in the compound over the course of nearly two hours laying in the dirt. No crimes are committed or clues are seen as to what is going on. Only the sentries appear to be armed. The others could have concealed handguns, but militias tend to be all about showing their toys off.

My phone vibrates in my pocket and I answer. "Eddie Holland." The conversation is short, and I hang up.

"Who was that?"

"The nurse in Salt Creek."

"What did she want?"

"She found some names of patients that came in bruised up like our dead friend."

"Did she tell you?"

"No. Didn't want to over the phone. We're going to meet her at the bar in town tonight."

"The bar. Like, there's only one?"

CHAPTER 5

We check into the one motel. It has a couple dozen rooms that I can't think are ever all booked at the same time. Salt Creek isn't a big convention town. We get connecting rooms and go our own ways to wash the desert off. Once clean, I relax on the bed in my underwear to air dry a bit and text Eva while the television plays *Storage Wars* in the background.

    - What are you wearing?

I watch the three blinking dots for far too long, hoping for a sexy, detailed description of her in something skimpy.

    - Green scrubs.

Right. She's at work. Could have at least played along with me. But she also knows when it's my turn I go straight to *Naked and ready*. I am not a man of mystery.

    - Are you boys behaving?

She knows us both well enough that she is likely sure we are sitting somewhere drinking beers and sharing FBI stories. Which is precisely what we'll be doing in just a few minutes.

- Just headed to the strip club.

- Oh? Visiting your ex-girlfriends?

- Yup. Hoping all my kids are there, too.

- Well have fun and make sure to give them each a dollar for all the birthdays you've missed.

- Love you.

- Love you, too :).

She gets me. I drop the phone onto the bed beside me and stare up at the water stains on the ceiling. At least I hope they're water stains. I can't count the number of shitty motels and hotels I've slept in over the years. This is far from the worst.

I change from my shorts into jeans and a ZZ Top T-shirt. No need to spook the locals with a band from anytime after 1989. Out of my room, I knock on Gus's door and he opens it wearing khakis and blue button-down.

"Dude. You get a job at Blockbuster?"

He looks at me. "Yeah. They pay better than your gig selling ironic T-shirts at Hot Topic."

I nod in approval.

The bar is two blocks down, past the out of business office supply store, the out of business hardware store, and the out of business diner. A bank that looks like it handles tens of dollars a day is the only thing that hasn't shuttered other than the bar.

Inside it is better than I expected, but I really expected

the worst, so anything is an improvement. The walls are all wood-paneled and the lights are a little too bright. A pool table in the back. A bar down the right wall and half a dozen tables. The CD juke box is playing "Legs" by ZZ Top. I punch Gus's arm.

"See, my shirt is not ironic."

We grab two beers and sit at a table where we can see the entire room. A short drunk man in overalls and no shirt is playing darts alone. He's clumping every dart he can find together and throwing them all at once. The third time he tries, one dart finds its way to the bullseye. The man turns around with a big smile on his face, pointing at the dart board, waiting for the mass celebration of his amazing accomplishment. It doesn't come.

"If this is a Wednesday night, imagine what Fridays are like," Gus says.

"I couldn't stand the excitement."

Gus and I have sat on stakeouts for hours and days together, hiked through mountains, and have been locked up in a safe house. There are not many topics we haven't talked about or secrets we haven't shared. We can sit in silence together or talk nonstop. Either is as comfortable as the other. I tease him hard, but he enjoys it.

"How's it going with Hope?" I ask. He started dating her less than a year ago and aside from one couples' date with us, keeps her to himself.

"Good. We're talking about taking a vacation soon."

"Like south coast of Texas vacation or a real vacation?"

"She wants to go to France."

"Oh, commitment level vacationing. Good for you!"

"Commitment level?" He gives me a puzzled look.

"You don't go to a country where they don't speak your language with someone you're dating casually. Even if it is exclusive."

"What are you talking about?"

"It's science. Being 4,000 miles from home with a pocket translator book, money you don't even know how to count in your wallet, and restaurants where you cannot read the menu is the ultimate test of a relationship. If you disagree whether to go to TGIFriday's or Red Robin at home, then everything you know is about to be tested."

"Science, eh."

"Science. Like Bill Nye level shit."

He smiles and sips from his beer bottle. "That her?"

Rebecca Morgan the Nurse looks around the small room and sees us. I wave her over.

I stand and she looks at me like she's confused why I'm standing. "Good to see you, Rebecca." I hope for the offer to call her Becks but again it doesn't come. What do you have to do?

"Thanks, I guess. Was surprised you were back in Salt Creek."

"It has a certain allure to it." I point at Gus. "This is Special Agent Gustavo Ramirez, the Mexican you talked to on the phone."

Gus turns his head to me so fast he should be in pain.

"Well, *hola* to you," she says.

"Um, hello," Gus says.

"We were following up on the info you gave me about Buster Ballard the other day," I say.

She looks around quickly. "Don't talk so loud. I'm not really supposed to share patient information."

"Why did you?" Gus asks.

"You see three or four people come in with the same bruises, similar tattoos, stuff like that, it makes you wonder."

We nod, giving her time to continue on her own.

"Then there's that place out east of town."

I avoid glancing at Gus. "That place?"

"That camp or whatever you wanna call it."

"Is that where all the men come from? The injured men?"

She nods.

"What do you know about the camp?" Gus says.

"Nobody knows much of nothing about it. Was just a bunch of deserted buildings until sometime last year. Then people started moving in, put up a fence."

"You know what goes on there?" I ask.

A head shake. "Some kind of religious group, most people say."

"Most people. What about you?"

"Look, I know we aren't the most progressive people out here you ever met. About everybody goes to church on Sunday, or if they can't, they have a Bible in their home. We vote Republican as the good Lord intended and try not to sin too much. But one thing that'll get people around here going is—" she looks around again then leans in, her voice coming out no quieter than it had been, "Satan worshippers."

Gus and I lean back at the same time and look at each other then back to Nurse Rebecca. Of all things she could have said, I had no money on Satan worshippers.

"I knew one of the guys that came into the hospital. The first one, several months ago. We went to junior high together. Hadn't seen him since then. Heard he's done some time and has a couple kids from a couple different moms around. But he isn't a bad guy."

"Did you talk to him when he was in the ER?" I say.

"Nothing beyond the usual. Don't know if he even recognized me. He was a year ahead of me back then."

"Why didn't you tell me about this when I first met you a couple weeks ago?"

She shrugs. "Didn't think it was important. Maybe a little embarrassed. Someone I know with those kinds of markings on 'em, living out in a camp with a bunch of other men."

"You said on the phone you have some more names."

"Yeah." She pulls a piece of paper out of her pocket and slides it over to me. "The first one is the guy I know. Or used to know, I guess."

A loud whooping sound comes from the door. Gus and I look up. Rebecca doesn't move or turn around to see. Six men come in, none of them too clean, all of them obnoxious. One yells to the bartender for two pitchers of beer and six shots and to "*Hurry the fuck up, will ya.*"

I look at Rebecca. "Is that them? Some of them?"

She looks quickly back toward the pool table where the men have pushed a young man and his girlfriend away, taking the quarters they had on the table.

"Yeah."

CHAPTER 6

I wake early but decide not to go for a run in the small town. I take a blanket from the second bed in my room and spread it on the floor, based on the idea that the blanket is slightly cleaner than the carpet, which looks like it came secondhand from a bankrupted Louisiana riverboat casino. After several dozen sit-ups, a hundred push-ups, and a few stretches, I hit the shower. Not long after that, I'm in the SUV with Gus headed south.

"Daryl Earl Chestnut." I read from the notes on Gus's phone. "Looks like everything Rebecca said about him is accurate, plus a few more times in jail than she knew about."

"He's no hardened criminal, but isn't as much of a good guy as she remembers," Gus says. "Aside from his visit to Salt Creek Regional Hospital a few months back, he's been off the grid for about a year."

"What are the chances he was one of the guys in the bar last night?"

"Don't know. Rebecca seemed pretty spooked by them, so she may not have pointed him out."

"You think it's Satan worshippers like she said?"

Gus shakes his head. "I don't know what to think, but that wouldn't be high on my list."

"Would be a first for me." I settle back into the passenger seat and watch the flat landscape roll by. Though Austin is my favorite part of the state, I've always had a thing for the flatness and emptiness out west. When here, it's easy to think about early settlers and people looking to make their fortunes on oil long before the big boom where there aren't high-rise buildings, traffic jams, and music festivals every other weekend to obscure the view and serenity. I'm always glad to get back to the city, though. And to Eva.

It's a 40-mile drive on a road with no curves to the last address on file for Daryl Chestnut. Gus stops on the shoulder and we both look down the long paved driveway that leads to a large brick house, a three-car garage to one side, and a swimming pool on the other. An arched sign over the driveway says 'Triple D Ranch."

"Triple D, eh. This could be interesting," I say. I can sense Gus's eye roll without looking at him. "Gotta admit I was expecting something more along the lines of a rusty trailer on blocks."

"Seemed more his style."

He turns down the drive. The grass on either side and in the long front yard to the road is bright green as arcing water sprinklers create rainbows that appear and disappear as we pass each spray. There's motion at the pool as Gus pulls to a stop. A woman stands up from a lounge chair and pulls a white robe over her sun-baked naked skin. We wait for her to come out of the wrought iron gate before approaching.

"Can I help you gentlemen?" She has the drawl of upper crust West Texas, the ones who got out for four years of college and came back to settle down and make money or live off their family fortunes. My guess is oil, but could be chickens.

"I'm Special Agent Gus Ramirez with the FBI. This is Eddie Holland."

"Should I call my attorney?" She has a smirk on her face and adjusts her robe, allowing more of a view than she realizes, or maybe she does realize. She's late-fifties probably, maybe early sixties, but hard to tell from the oven roasted skin.

"No, ma'am," Gus says. "Are you Debra Chestnut?"

"The one and only." Everything she says sounds like a flirt and I can't say it doesn't work.

"Is your son Daryl here?"

"Sounds like he's stepping up in the world. The FBI? What has he done now?"

"Nothing, ma'am, we—"

"Oh, stop calling me ma'am before I spank you like your momma never did," she says. "Debra is fine, or Ms. Chestnut if you're uncomfortable being sociable. Someone called my momma ma'am once and she smacked them upside the head with a stick."

"She sounds like she was a pleasant woman," I say.

"She was, right up to the day she killed my daddy with a station wagon."

We both stare at Debra Chestnut, not knowing if she is joking.

"Pull your jaws back up, boys, and tell me what you need with my son."

"We're looking into a series of cases that came through the hospital up in Salt Creek," Gus says. "Over the last six months or so, several men have been in with excessive bruising and cuts. One man recently died with similar injuries."

"Is my Daryl alive?" She looks serious for the first time.

"Yes ma'— Ms. Chestnut," Gus says. "He was treated and released from the hospital. We haven't spoken with him because we don't have a current address for him."

"He still gets his mail here, but I haven't seen him in ages."

"Can you tell us anything about him, people he was hanging out with or involved with?"

"What, like a gang or a cult or something?" She turns back to the pool with a swing of the head to tell us to follow. I hold open the gate for her and Gus. "He's never had the best of luck with friends. First time he went to jail was covering for a boy who had robbed a liquor store. Damn fools didn't even look anything alike, but the police took his word it was him. By the time he was out, the other boy was long gone."

Debra picks up a glass from a table beside the lounge chair she was on when we arrived and took a long drink of water. "I'm sorry I don't have any extra glasses out here.

I can run in and get some if you are going to be lingering much longer."

"That's fine, Debra," I say. "You've been very helpful."

Gus pulls a card out of his wallet. "If you think of anything that could be helpful, or hear from Daryl, would you give us a call?"

"Certainly, Special Agent Ramirez." She reads his name aloud from the card. "Now if you don't mind, I'd like to get in a little more sun before it gets too hot out here."

Before we can turn away, she has her robe open and it drops to the ground. She pauses in her nudity before us, either to impress or scare us off, I'm not sure.

"Thank you, Ms. Chestnut," Gus says. "Have a pleasant day." He would have tipped his hat if he had one.

We turn and walk away, doing our best not to look back. Once in the SUV we see her still standing and watching us. An arm comes up and gives a flick of the wrist in waving goodbye, then she sits and reclines back onto the lounge chair.

Gus backs up and points the SUV down the driveway.

"Well, I think we can safely say there is one thing we learned here," I say.

"What's that?"

"Triple D Ranch is not named after her."

CHAPTER 7

There is only a sliver of moon an hour after sunset and the plains are painted in shades of black. The headlights of the SUV barely make a dent in the night as we drive back out toward the compound from Salt Creek. It is silent in the car. Music would disturb the darkness, and make the transition to the outside world more jarring. I look forward to the sounds of the plains at night. The sky acts as an echo chamber for everything on the ground, amplifying.

We reach the turn we took yesterday and Gus slows down as we enter the field. We had walked in before and he felt he could drive us closer to avoid the trek on foot in the dark, to have the relative safety of the SUV nearer to us. It's bumpy and scraping noises come from beneath us as we go over scraggly bushes that struggle to live in the dry and hot soil. He turns the headlights off and the dash lights are so bright in contrast to outside the truck that he quickly finds the dial to turn them off.

Rolling in complete darkness, I bring down my window to get more connected to the world. There is no moisture. No humidity at all. The air feels rough against my arm as I stretch it out through the opening.

Gus stops.

"Think this is it?" I speak softly and it is still too loud for the surroundings.

"Yeah. Pretty damn close." He turns the engine off and the quiet is deafening. "I counted the rises in the land when we were walking back yesterday. There were five, and we just came up our fifth since where we parked."

"Works for me."

Neither of us slam our doors, closing them softly, then pushing them the final bit until they latch. Gus leaves the truck unlocked to avoid the flashing of lights and beep from the horn. Sound travels great distances out here and we don't need to broadcast our arrival.

We stay close, Gus in front again. We both have flashlights but try not to use them. I hold mine in my hand. A sort of security blanket. A blunt force weapon. My Glock is on my hip, and Gus has his Sig, but those seem out of place with no actual threat of violence.

With the cover of night, we don't duck down when we reach the final ridge. The ground for a few hundred yards ahead is as dark as that behind us.

The buildings of the compound glow just beyond. Small lights come from the windows of the few small buildings and trailer. But the main source of light is from the bonfire in the center. The flames lick high into the air and even from a distance I can make out the sparks coming off the tips and floating out into the air and down to the ground.

Men are sitting on stumps and chairs on one side of the fire. I count ten. Two more are lazily walking the border of the camp at the edge where light goes to dark, the assault rifles slung low across their backs.

"I see twelve," Gus says.

"Same. The sentries are sloppy."

"They are."

"I don't see much Satan worshipping going on."

"Maybe they're subtle about it."

"Could be."

Some of the men get up and move around the fire. Nobody appears to be drinking or disorderly. Definitely no fighting that would cause the bruises I'd seen on Buster Ballard's dead body.

"Maybe it's just better than being homeless." I scan my binoculars around to get a closer look at the buildings. "They could just be living together for company, protection."

"Homeless people don't tend to have AR-15s. Even in Texas."

"You have a point," I say.

"Hmm," Gus says.

"Hmm what?"

"I only count eight now."

I look again. "You're right. Sentries have their rifles tightened up in front now, too."

I turn to Gus as I listen to the air. Something is different. A whine, a dissonance to the sounds of the outside. His eyes go wide just as we both figure it out.

The engine sound gets louder, going from low speed to an aggressive roar, but we can't tell from where as we both move backward slowly, heads moving to take in everything we can.

"Sounds like at least two, unless it's just echoing," I say.

"I think we should get to the SUV," Gus says.

"I concur, wholeheartedly."

We've taken no more than ten steps back toward the Explorer when headlights and bright searchlights come on from either side of us, still a good quarter mile away.

"Don't use your flashlight. They'll be able to see us," Gus says.

"Don't have to tell me twice."

We're moving through the brush as fast as we can with no visibility. I trip once then Gus does. The rattlesnake we saw yesterday is fresh in my mind. It's only a few dozen yards to the SUV and he climbs in behind the steering wheel. I get in the back seat.

"Think you can get us out of here in the dark?"

Gus turns the dial on the console to switch to four-wheel-drive, then cranks the wheel and starts to move. "I'm sure as hell gonna try."

I'm unbelted and bouncing around on my knees as I search all directions for the lights. The navigation screen lights up and shows us in the middle of the field, the thin line of the farm road directly behind us a few hundred yards. Gus watches the screen as much as he does the darkness outside.

"I don't see them."

"Me either," he says. "Keep looking."

I have both back windows down to listen for the engines. Then I'm blinded by at least six huge lights from forty feet away. Gus punches the gas with the view ahead of him lit up and I fly backwards in the seat.

"Dammit!"

"Sorry."

The lights go out again.

"They're pinging us." The lights go on and off from either side for only a second or two at a time, enough to allow the drivers to locate us and readjust course, just as a submarine pings with sonar to search for ships and other subs in the ocean. I face the back of the SUV and squint to make out any shapes moving in the darkness. A shadow sticks out for a moment then is gone.

"There's one five o'clock. I think."

"You think?" He turns left hard and I go flying again, then pull myself back up.

Gus is plowing over bushes and who knows what else when the lights come on straight ahead and coming at us fast.

"Shit! I can't see a damn thing!" he yells.

"Stay the course! Speed up."

"You want me to play chicken with them?"

"Why not?"

The SUV lurches forward with the painful sound of scraping beneath us and the engine revving high in the loose dirt, fighting to keep traction. The lights get brighter as we close the distance.

"He'll go to our left," I say.

"Why do you think that?"

"Just a guess. Keep going!"

The inside of our SUV is lit up like daylight with the vehicle traveling at us fast. Gus has his sun visor down trying to keep from being blinded.

"Almost there. Keep on it, Gus."

He does and moments before we should impact, the vehicle coming at us takes a hard turn right, going off to our left.

"Get us out of here."

"Where's the other one?"

The other lights come on and illuminate the vehicle we just played chicken with. I see the broad side of a red Chevy pickup with a roll bar lined with high powered lights.

"Doesn't even look like a four by four so they're probably struggling out here," I say.

"They seem to be keeping up just fine," Gus says.

He finds the entrance to the farm road and has his headlights on and the SUV up to 80 miles per hour in no time and keeps accelerating. I sit and buckle myself in the backseat.

Salt Creek comes up fast at speed and he enters town at triple the marked thirty miles per hour limit, having the knowledge that there's no local police force. We pass the bar and our motel and he turns left onto one of the few side streets. In the alley behind the motel, he finds a battered green trash dumpster and parks the SUV beside it away from the light.

On the walk to the front of the motel, we stay in shadows where possible. I fight the urge to pull my Glock and hold it. As we approach the corner of the building, I pause and

Gus stops behind me. The red Chevy drives by followed by a black Ford pickup with the same setup of lights on a roll bar. The windows are down and we see two men in each cab. Once they are down the road, we get up the stairs and into our rooms. I open the connecting door to his room, and he does, too.

I go to bed as I have so many times with my Glock under the other pillow. It's at least an hour until I fall asleep while listening for noises outside the room.

CHAPTER 8

I'm up before dawn again and peaking through the dusty blinds to the outside world. The air is yellow from a storm moving in. The dust and pollen blows around casting an eerie glow to the already surreal feel of the west Texas ghost town. I'm ready to get out of here.

Gus comes through the connecting door to his room with a small overnight bag in his hand. I grab my backpack and we leave. A few heavy raindrops hit us as we walk down the sidewalk, seconds between each, leaving big round wet spots on the ground. The impending storm is getting closer.

The SUV is still behind the motel. He inspects the side to find the scratches from the brush scraping against it in our late night adventure. The black paint is coated in brown and yellow dust.

"It'll buff out," I say.

He doesn't respond. With the engine started, he points the vehicle down the road and passes the turn to the highway. More rain on the windshield, but not enough for the wipers yet. I turn and look longingly at the on ramp behind us.

"Hey there, buddy," I speak softly. "Where ya goin'?"

"We're already out here, might as well take one more look."

I look over at him. "Have you gone completely batshit crazy?"

Silence seems to be his standard reply this morning, so I settle in for the drive back to the compound and think about what happened last night and hope we don't have a repeat. I could argue more, but I know how Gus is when he's made his mind up.

He drives into the field we raced through last night without slowing down and doesn't stop to hike the last few hundred yards as we did the first day. He drives right up to the edge of the ridge and stops, not caring if we are seen. He doesn't ask my opinion on this but I'll always support him.

We grab our binoculars and look. There are two sentries with AR-15s across their chests, ready for action. Two other men with sidearms are with them. The two pickups are parked longways across the inside of the sliding gate.

"We definitely spooked them."

More silence. I know it isn't directed at me. I've pissed Gus off before and know exactly what that is like. This is different. This is full concentration on a case, on filtering through his experiences and observations, and what we've learned. This isn't going to end here.

Gus Ramirez was one of the few kids in fifth grade that wasn't white. In Austin, that's rare. He grew up a few streets from me. His father was a bank manager and his mother a teacher across town. He never thought of himself as different. But that year it changed. Several boys teased him for being Mexican. I'm not proud to admit that I was one of them. I can't say I didn't know better. I did. At first I was going along with the cool guys, just having fun, trying to fit in. As soon as I saw that Gus didn't think it was funny, I felt like shit and switched sides. I've had his back since that day. We had it out over, don't get me wrong. I had to earn his trust. But by end of that year we were inseparable and after a few quick strike bloody noses that happened so fast no teachers saw them, nobody bullied Gus again. From then on we didn't care about being the cool kids or the losers. We were just us.

Through the binoculars I see one of the sentries look right at us. He doesn't move his rifle or signal to everyone else. He just stares at us. From this distance we are a small black dot of the SUV and two blurry figures looking back at him. But still he stares.

"Let's go," Gus says.

The sky opens up as we walk back to the Ford Explorer. The dusty ground turns to mud quickly and Gus pushes down harder on the gas just to speed through it. I watch behind us for signs of the red or black pickup, but nobody is giving chase. They had their fun with us last night.

An hour into the drive, Gus turns off into a small town and pulls into one of the three Sonics he had located on our route. It's early for lunch, but the staff is happy to accommodate. A burger, cherry limeade with light ice, and two orders of tater tots later and Gus is closer to his normal self.

"Any thoughts?" I try to open conversation.

He chews and looks out the driver's door window. "Best guess is militia. Possibly white supremacists, but there was at least one Mexican guy in the camp, so I don't think so."

"Saw him, too."

"There's still a dead body sitting back in Salt Creek with nobody to claim him."

"And you think state police or Texas Rangers would do nothing?"

He nods. "They want cases handed over to them with bows on top, all tied up and ready to prosecute someone. Otherwise they have no interest. It's all about closed cases for them, not closing cases."

"Do you have any jurisdiction over this or enough of a case to claim it?"

"I'm working on that. A dead body isn't enough. The swastikas on Buster Ballard help. Anything white supremacist related has the possibility to go federal. Local PDs don't care about that as much since they don't have their own laws to cover it."

"I have a feeling we'll be back in Salt Creek soon," I say.

He doesn't respond while taking a drink from his cherry limeade.

That's Gus. He will lose sleep and fight to open an investigation into a dead boy with swastikas and white nationalist tattoos, because it's the right thing to do. And that's why he's my best friend.

I let him choose the music and I pretended to sleep the rest of the drive while secretly enjoying the podcast on the declining population of honeybees in the world.

CHAPTER 9

Eva is at work when Gus drops me off. I texted her earlier on the drive and she said she'll be home by seven. That gives me several hours alone.

I start with a shower that lasts nearly thirty minutes. The water that started at a scalding temperature is reduced to luke warm by the time I give in and turn it off. After drying and pulling on some underwear, I consider my options. I can grab a beer and sit on the balcony and enjoy the afternoon, turn on the television and lose some brain cells to *Storage Wars* and *American Pickers*, or put some Bob Seger on the stereo and reenact Tom Cruise's dance scene from *Risky Business* on the living room hardwood floors.

The beer is cold and the air is hot on the balcony, and I love it. Leaning back in the chair just far enough I can still sip without spilling. I do my best not to think about the last two days. There will be time for that tomorrow when I regroup with Gus.

I call the bar to check on them and everything is set for a small acoustic show tonight. That's always a quiet crowd and a lot of craft beer sold, which isn't as good for profits than Miller Lite from the tap, but money is money.

Starting at six o'clock, I begin checking the time every few minutes in anticipation of Eva getting home. I haven't seen her in two days and that is two too many. She's getting off a twelve-hour shift in the Emergency Room and will be tired and hungry. She works too hard but she doesn't know any other way.

By the time she walks through the door from the garage, I'm in jeans, a nice shirt, and a blue plaid duckbill cap. I wrap my arms around her and hold her head to my shoulder.

"Mmm. You smell good," she says.

"You smell like sick people."

"So many sick people," she says. "We need a proper vacation."

"Soon."

She steps back and looks at me, clean and dressed. "You really wanna go out, I can tell."

"I was thinking somewhere nice and romantic, a table outside, a bottle of wine..."

She looks up at me with feigned excitement. "Sure. Just let me shower first."

The doorbell rings and she looks over her shoulder.

"Who on earth could that be?"

"Oh, that's a couple of Greek Sicilian pizzas from Milto's. There's a bottle of wine open in the kitchen. We aren't going anywhere."

Eva falls into my chest. "Oh, I love you."

"And did I mention the cannoli?"

Her arms tighten around me.

She heads upstairs to take a shower as I get the food and put it in the oven to stay warm. By the time she comes down, I've changed into shorts and a T-shirt and she's in her comfy pajamas with no bra on which always makes me smile.

We eat on the living room floor, our favorite place to sit and talk. She doesn't ask questions about the trip back to Salt Creek. She always waits until I bring up a case, knowing I need time to process before I talk through it out loud with her. More than a few times she's helped me focus in on whatever I was missing.

"Where do you want to go?" I say.

"On vacation? Well. I would like to go farther than Padre. Maybe San Diego. Or Mexico."

"Definitely somewhere beachy?"

"Yes, but with other stuff to do."

"How about an island?" I say.

"Like St. Thomas, perhaps?" she says.

I nod as I consider all the options. "Soon, I hope. Once I see what's going on with this case that isn't really a case, we'll book something and go."

"Promise?"

"Promise. Be ready to tell the hospital you will be gone for two days."

She turns and looks at me. "Two days?"

"Oh, you want longer?"

She pretends to hit me in the stomach, instead falling

onto me and I hold her in my arms. I would do anything for this woman, but sometimes I'm a little slow to do it. I get wrapped up in my work and lose track of time, lose sight of what's important. In the end, the most important thing to me is her. The bar can manage without me. I don't have to take every case that comes along.

"I've been thinking." She says it as if she is still processing her thoughts.

"About?"

"Making a change from the E.R."

She's mentioned it before, but in the end she enjoys it too much. It's the front lines of medicine, a literal life or death situation almost every day. She thrives on that and is excellent at it. But it takes a toll on her. You can't win every time and when she loses someone, it puts her in a funk for several days.

"Whatever you want, you know that. Whenever you're ready, I'm sure you know who to talk to."

"That's the thing." She sits up and turns to face me on the floor. "I didn't have to reach out. Somebody already called me."

"Oh, really?"

She nods. "There's a private practice that has a great reputation. They have a dozen staff doctors then another dozen or so who rotate in from the university. It's a teaching practice. But I know a couple of the partners, and they're interested in introducing me to the rest of the founders. I'm actually meeting them for coffee in the morning to talk more."

"That sounds amazing."

"I know."

"So, are you going to do it?"

She looks over my shoulder at nothing in particular. She's gone for a moment, lost in the perpetual list of pros and cons she keeps in the back of her thoughts. She keeps her world organized in there somehow. At any time you can ask about her patients and she knows what is going on with each of them. House bills are taken care of before I ever get a chance to see them. She gets the oil changed on her car before it is even due.

"Yeah." She smiles and looks back at me. "If it all looks good, I am."

The night progresses from talking about her future to kissing to moving our party up to the bedroom.

CHAPTER 10

I wake before the sun is up and pull shorts on for a run. My grey Brooks Adrenaline shoes are by the back door. As I stop to pull them on, I glance through the window to the darkness and consider getting a jacket or even a sweatshirt. Two steps through the door, though, the 85-degree temperature hits me and I almost laugh for thinking it might be chilly in Austin on a summer morning.

There's no traffic on Martin Luther King Boulevard this early and I take the right line as my path. I cross over 183 and the smell of the breakfast meats cooking at Burger King fill my nose and make me instantly hungry. Good thing I don't run with money on me or I'd be stopping to eat. The worst part is I know a couple miles down I have to go right between a Popeye's and a Whattaburger.

Running is when I do my best thinking. I'm not as

mentally organized as Eva, so it takes me time to put all the parts together. There's not enough of this case yet to try to assemble. It's a two-piece puzzle with one of the pieces missing. So instead I think of Eva and speed my pace to hopefully catch her in the shower.

I survive the run without begging at a drive-through window for a sausage biscuit and go straight to the kitchen when I get home and fry myself two eggs and lightly toast a piece of bread. I sit at the counter and commend myself for surviving the fast food gauntlet.

Eva is still asleep as I go through the bedroom. I slide the bathroom door closed behind me, drop my shorts to the floor, and step into the shower before the water has warmed up, a post run ritual that wakes my skin and brain. Before long, the steam is kicking up and I stand with my face aimed up at the nozzle, letting it soak me.

"Can I get your back?"

I startle and turn to see Eva stepping into the oversized shower with me, her pajamas left somewhere between here and the bed.

"You can even get my front, little lady."

And she does.

After the shower, I'm dried and dressed in minutes then sit on the bed and watch her get ready. Most days she's almost as fast as I am, unless she has to dry her hair. She gets the blow dryer out and plugs it in.

"Nervous?"

She turns, her bathrobe loose in front and revealing a sliver of her body to me. I just had full access in the shower and still it excites me.

"Trying not to be." She sits next to me, her hands fidgeting with the blow dryer. "I've known these two guys for years. One used to work in the E.R. with me, so it isn't that big a deal. Just thinking about meeting the rest of them is kinda nerve racking, though. For one, it will let the cat out of the bag that I'm looking. Austin isn't a big city, and most people in the profession know each other, or at least of each other. Won't take long for administration at the hospital to get wind of it."

"It's like the bureau. Talk to a SAC from a field office on the other side of the country about possibly transferring there and five minutes later you have a dozen agents looking at you like you're defecting."

"Exactly."

"Don't worry about them. You do what's best for you."

"I know. Thanks." She leans her head on my shoulder for a moment then moves back to the bathroom to dry her hair.

I grab two coffees at the deli down the street from Gus's building and carry them up. He's sitting behind his desk, the usual stack of paperwork in front of him. He sees the cups and practically grabs one out of my hand.

"Oh sweet milk of the heavens, thank you, thank you." He sips from the cup then leans his head back like an addict that just took a hit.

"You might have a problem."

"Didn't sleep last night. I'm jittery and seeing double this morning."

"Caffeine should definitely help that."

"This is my third cup."

"Why no sleep? A new case? Our Salt Creek situation?"

He looks over the top of the cup at me while taking a bigger drink.

"Ohhh. Right. Let me think." I count the months in my head. "It's been a year, right?"

"Yup. Hope and I celebrated last night with far too many margaritas on a school night, followed by, well, not sleeping."

"Go get 'em, tiger."

"Thanks. So, since you mentioned it, I have some info about Salt Creek."

"Do tell."

"I did a little digging into the compound. The lot is being rented by a company called Ruby Rising, LLC."

"Rented?"

"Yup. Month-to-month. Another property came up being owned by Ruby Rising, LLC, and it happens to be just down the road from the compound."

"Another militia group?"

"No. The second one is a ranch. About three hundred acres. Doesn't appear to have livestock or crops or anything else."

"How long have they owned it?"

"Twenty years."

"What's the LLC's deal?"

"The actual LLC is a newer thing. Paperwork was filed in Delaware through one of those do-it-yourself websites. Ownership of the ranch was transferred into the LLC a short time after."

"Ruby Rising." I say it out loud, more to myself than for anyone else.

"Sound familiar?"

"Something about it, yeah. What's next?"

"I'm down at the field office in San Antonio tomorrow for some briefings. Going to chat with the SAC about it, see if there's anything worth following up on or just letting the state police deal with Buster Ballard's body."

"How do you feel about that?"

"You know me. I want to see it through, but if there isn't anything there for the bureau, then the files get transferred to state police or the Rangers."

"If it does go away, you did what you could, and far more than what would have happened if anyone but you had gotten that tip line call."

CHAPTER 11

Clem Akins hands me one end of a sheet of plywood he just cut. I hold it in place as he hammers several nails through in single strikes until it is flush with the other pieces we already put up on the side of the addition to his small house out in the country near Killeen, Texas. Clem stands back to admire the work.

"Looks good, Eddie."

"I'm just the helper, Clem."

"All right. Let's start on the next side."

"Whoa. Don't you ever take a break? I seem to recall the deal was help a while then drink some cold beers a while."

He looks up at the last of the three sides to complete the bump-out on his long, narrow house, then nods.

"Beer sounds good," he says.

We move to the back yard and I follow him down the

three steps into the old tornado shelter he's turned into a fully armed bunker. He holds the wall with one hand while favoring his left leg on the stairs.

"You doing okay there?"

"I am. The lining of the socket has worn down in a couple places and it's rubbing my nub raw." He reaches down and touches the rounded area of his prosthetic leg where what's left of his thigh fits down into it.

Before I knew Clem, at least before we met, I had watched on a large screen deep inside a secure building in the Virginia suburbs of Washington, D.C. as he led a team of Army Rangers into a raid of a village in Afghanistan. Three soldiers were left dead, and Clem was flown home missing a leg, ending his time in the field as a Ranger.

"I'm sure they can fix that for you," I say. "Maybe even get a brand new one. New technology. Maybe bionic."

"I don't need anything bionic. I'm already stronger than you."

"That you are, and can probably outrun me."

"Probably?"

He hands me a Shiner and we sit in the only two chairs in the small, cement room. It's easily twenty degrees cooler in the partially submerged cement shelter than outside, and that's without the Mitsubishi air conditioner unit he retrofitted into the structure.

The wall in front of us is covered in weapons, each secure on pegs and evenly spaced. There's at least a hundred pistols and rifles of all size and shape. Each one has a bright orange trigger lock and, knowing Clem, the larger caliber weapons have the firing pin removed for extra caution. The lock boxes on the floor beneath the guns are full of ammunition for each and every one of them. There's even a flintlock blunderbuss with the flared barrel that he claims was from the Irish military in the late 1800's and never fired.

"What's been keeping you busy, my friend?" He reaches his beer bottle over and we tap the necks.

"Working a case with Gus, as usual. At least we think it's a case. We're not really sure yet."

I fill him in on some of the details. He nods along as I do. When I finish, he's silent for a minute.

"Nobody deserves to die a useless death," he says. "And nobody deserves to have someone die and they don't know why or how. Somewhere out there is someone who is missing him."

I take a long drink of the beer.

"I personally visited the homes of eight of my soldiers. I sat there and talked to parents and grandparents and brothers and sisters of men that died under my command. I didn't have to. Letters are sent from D.C. They get calls from their Senators, if not the President. The arrangements are made for them. But those families deserved to hear from me."

"This isn't a soldier who served under me or Gus," I say. "It's a kid with a long rap sheet and swastika inked all over his skin."

"But his family is still out there, and right now, you and Gus are the only people he has that can do anything about getting answers. The boy was a dumbshit, sure. But it's about his family now."

I know he's right. It's the direction I already wanted to

go, but hearing it from Clem solidifies it. Buster Ballard deserves better than what the state police or Texas Rangers will do for him.

I stop after two beers, and still hang out an extra hour before leaving to make sure I'm okay to drive before I get in Eva's Fiat and head back down to Austin. I think about everything Clem said while I let the evening air blast through the open windows as the underpowered stereo struggles to play White Denim's album *Stiff* over the roar of the wind.

I believe in the sanctity of the album. Each song played in order as the artist chose them to be. Would you play Pink Floyd's *The Wall* on shuffle? I think not. There's a flow that's intended, musically and lyrically, to every album. Ask anyone who grew up before iPods and MP3s if when they hear certain songs and the final notes fade out, there isn't a song they expect to hear right after it. Fleetwood Mac's "Never Going Back Again" is incomplete if it doesn't roll right into "Don't Stop." The title track of *Bat Out of Hell* by Meat Loaf has to be followed by the Jim Steinman narrated opening of "You Took the Words Right Out of My Mouth" or it just isn't right.

Traffic is light and I park behind Buddy's Music Tavern and let myself in the back door. I can hear the first band playing on stage through the wall in my office. They sound sloppy and inexperienced, but it's their first real gig that isn't in a garage or a friend's basement. The main act later is the draw for tonight, a local favorite who will be too big to play in my bar within the year.

I step through the curtain out of the back room and see the three boys on stage trying their hardest to keep up with each other. The bass player looks smaller than the instrument he's holding. At the bar I motion for a beer and Vincent, my club manager and bartender, brings me whatever new he has for me to try out. He's older than me by a couple decades. I offered a partnership to him once, ownership in the club, and he laughed at me and replied with, "Fuck that shit." Even at his age, it's about the music and the crowds and not being tied down. His wife and four kids, two in college, might have something different to say about that.

"What do you think?" I motion to the stage with my head without turning around.

He looks over my shoulder, then back at me, and the eye roll says it all. He's seen more bands come and go than most people in Austin. Rumor has it he called a guy he knew, who called another guy who knew a rep at Matador Records when he saw an early gig by Spoon. There is a framed photo of him and lead singer Britt Daniel hanging behind the bar. He was working at Antone's when Stevie Ray Vaughan and Double Trouble blew audience's minds before making it huge. There's not a better man to have behind my bar and running the bookings while I'm off playing secret agent or photographing golf-playing businessmen who are supposed to have whiplash from a five mile per hour bump in a company car.

My phone vibrates. A text from Gus.

Where are you?

The bar, I respond.

I'll be there in 10.

I tell Vincent to send Gus back to my office and to give him whatever he wants to drink on the way. He responds with a dismissive raise of his chin which from Vincent means he's thinking about thirty other things right then and will no doubt still remember everything I ask of him.

I'm browsing a classic car website when Gus walks in, beer in hand. He pulls the only other chair closer and sits down next to me.

"May I help you?" He's inches away and doesn't look good.

He stares at me for a long time, then starts talking and doesn't stop for fifteen minutes.

CHAPTER 12

I'm leaning back in my chair, one foot on the edge of my desk supporting me. It is an unfortunate position to be in when I hear what Gus has to say. I lean forward, the legs of the solid metal grey chair slam to the floor.

"He wants me to what?"

"I know, I know. I tried to talk him out of it. To pull an agent from San Antonio or Dallas, but he says he wants you."

"Why me?"

"He wants someone with plausible deniability if things turn south."

"The FBI puts agents undercover every single day. It's what they do." I feel a pit in my stomach. Or an ulcer. Something bad, whatever it is.

Gus can only nod in agreement. "There's concern over

militias growing in power, especially here in Texas. Almost every field office is dealing with this, but most don't have a lead into them to get someone inside. It's the fear over domestic terrorism. The bureau doesn't want another Waco or Oklahoma City."

I look at Gus. "Or Ruby Ridge." The 1992 siege in Ruby Ridge, Idaho, lasted eleven days as U.S. Marshals attempted to arrest a man named Randy Weaver on firearms charges.

He leans back and stares at me. "Ruby Ridge. Ruby Rising."

Everything that had seemed odd or familiar about Ruby Rising when we first learned about the LLC suddenly clicked. If we were talking about a local gang breaking into cars, I wouldn't have thought anything of it. But we have what resembles a militia with white supremacist ties.

"Coincidence?" I try to convince myself it is. "Has to be a coincidence."

Gus is shaking his head. "It's too much to be a coincidence, but I hope it is."

I feel we both know it isn't. I push my foot against the desk again, front legs of the chair lifting off the taupe carpet, and I stare up at the ceiling. Something is hiding, trying to come forward. A piece of information, a memory, a word. *Ruby Rising.* I roll it around some more.

"Even so, what does the SAC think the bureau has? There's a body on a slab in Salt Creek. That's it. And since when did militias start incorporating?"

"It's actually become more common as a way to look legitimate, to buy weapons almost anonymously, order supplies."

"Like fertilizer?"

"Like fertilizer."

"I guess there is a reason, then. But does it have to be me? Tell him I have a vacation planned or I've developed narcolepsy."

"This is why you still have your badge, Eddie. It's how you're still on the inside while staying outside at the same time. This is the price for unfettered access to the bureau's resources. To me."

"You're pretty damn expensive."

"I'm worth it."

We sip our beers and I step out to motion for Vincent to bring us two more. He's right. I hate to admit it. I've flown too close to the bureaucratic sun for years now without the wax melting. No meetings. No suits. No *yes sirs*.

"What's next, then?"

Gus glances at his watch. "In about seven hours we're wheels up to Yuma."

"Yuma?"

"One of the names your nurse friend provided gave us a hit on an address. Turns out to be a vacant lot that used to be an airport. I talked to a detective there and he said it was a couple trailers just east of downtown. They were there a few months. Big bonfire every night. Some reports of fights, but nothing outside their camp that he knew of."

"You talk to any hospitals there?" I say.

"Not yet. We'll do that on the ground while we're there," Gus says. "Let you use that Eddie Holland charm that worked so well on the nurse from Salt Creek."

"No other activities from them while there?"

"No. SAC Hudson thinks drugs, of course, since they were right by the border and still aren't too far."

"Drugs? Importing, exporting, or using?"

"Most likely importing, and probably distributing. He wants us to check it out before we get you ready for militia life."

"Great."

I wait out my three beers while staring at the computer screen without really seeing it and listening to the thumping of the drums through the wall. Gus only had one and headed home. *Ruby Rising*. There's something there. Something I'm forgetting or missing.

Eva is asleep when I get home. I double check my phone. No angry texts about picking her up. She must have gotten a ride or taken an Uber. Still dirty from working on Clem's house and smelly from being at the bar drinking with Gus, I jump in the shower and wash off. Shortly after, I'm climbing into bed.

I pull the covers over me as slowly as possible to not disturb her. I already have to tell her first thing in the morning that I'm going to Yuma for a couple days. Last thing I need is to upset her now.

As soon as I settle in on my back, her hand lands on my chest.

"What's going on?" she says.

"Nothing we can't talk about in the morning."

She lifts her head to see the clock on my nightstand. One-fifteen.

"It's morning."

"It isn't that big a deal. Gus and I have to fly to Arizona for a couple days to follow up on a case."

"Arizona?" Her voice is muffled in the pillow.

"Yuma. It's about that body we stopped to see."

"What else?"

Dammit. How does she do this?

"Well, after we get back, I'll be going back out to Salt Creek for a while."

"What's a while mean?"

"A few days. A week. I'm not sure yet."

She sits up in bed, going from mostly asleep to completely awake in a millisecond. It must be a doctor thing.

"Are you going under?"

This is what I get for dating a cop's daughter.

"I wouldn't say—"

"Dammit, Eddie. I don't like this. Going off tq Yuma or other places for a day or two with Gus is one thing. But undercover with white supremacists?"

"We don't know if—"

"He was covered in swastikas, Eddie."

"True, but—"

"Swastikas."

"Yes. He was." I can't beat her in an argument, especially when she's simply looking out for my safety. "I'll be careful. Gus will be nearby the whole time."

"Will you have your gun?"

"Not at first, probably. But you know me. I'll find a way."

Her hand goes back to my chest as she lies down beside me, then rolls over and I pull in behind her, holding her close to me. She's asleep in moments. Damn her.

I stare up into the darkness and run it though my mind some more. *Ruby Rising*. The beers and the exhaustion from the day take my body and relax my brain. As I fade to sleep I see a hooded shape in the darkness and hear the words so clearly as if they were being spoken out loud in our bedroom.

"*The ruby rising in the east.*"

CHAPTER 13

I walk behind Gus down the jetway at Austin-Bergstrom airport to board our flight to Yuma.

"Couldn't you get one of your private planes this time?"

"Nobody was headed this way."

"Does anybody head this way?"

"If they're going to San Diego, but then they just fly right over Yuma."

"True."

We were able to bypass security to clear our guns with the air marshall since we are on official business, otherwise the pistols would be broken down in locked cases underneath the plane with regular luggage. It's important to keep them concealed during the flight. Guns tend to spook passengers, even if they are on federal agents. But I guess they don't know we're federal agents. My Pantera concert T-shirt from

1997 probably doesn't instill much confidence.

By the time we land, Gus has watched an Anne Hathaway movie on the headrest screen, and I've pretended to sleep while watching the same Anne Hathaway movie.

Being from Austin, we're used to heat. We live in it most of the year and make do even in the hottest weeks. Music festivals still go on. Pools are open. Kids play summer sports outside. But walking out of the airport in Yuma, Arizona, is a pure sensation of entering the pits of hell. The heat hits us like a wall, sucking the oxygen from the air we're trying to breathe. We both come to a stop as the doors slide behind us.

"What in the living hell?" Gus says. "I've never felt anything like this."

"It's what I imagine a potato feels like when I'm baking it in the oven, except hotter."

We pick up a white Dodge Durango at the rental car company and head into Yuma. Even with the air conditioner turned up full blast, our shirts are both still soaked through with sweat, and not drying.

Within a few minutes, we're parked at the police station and inhaling deep breaths before opening the doors to make the dash inside.

"Detective Morales, please." Gus turns away from the counter. The pit stains on his light blue FBI polo shirt look like they could be wrung out, not that I'd touch them.

"Special Agent Ramirez?"

A very tall and wide man walks up to us. He has a white short sleeve button down shirt tucked into blue jeans. The thought of jeans outside here almost makes me collapse from heat stroke. My cargo shorts are too hot for me.

"Detective Rafael Morales." Gus and the detective shake hands and exchange the usual pleasantries. *Honor to help the FBI. Thank you for your department's assistance.*

"Call me Raf."

The detective leads us to a meeting room off the main lobby and pulls a roll-up map down of greater Yuma. He motions to an area southeast of the city.

"This is where we're going," he says. "It's about forty miles away. It isn't part of Yuma, but state police are spread thin and we help them out wherever we can. There were three travel trailers there at one point. Two of them were left behind and the city towed them to impound."

"You still have them?" Gus says.

"They were sold off at auction a few weeks ago."

"That's unfortunate," I say.

"We went through them thoroughly. Even had some new officers use them for practice to lift prints, but they came up with nothing. Both had been completely wiped down."

"Didn't that raise some flags?" Gus says.

"It did, but by then the other trailer and all the men that had been living at the site were gone. We ran the plates we had but got no hits."

"You put out a BOLO?" Gus says, asking about the general "be on the lookout" request police forces can put out for other law enforcement to watch for people or vehicles.

"To be honest, didn't have a reason to," Raf says. "Plus, like I said, it isn't even our jurisdiction."

"I understand," Gus says. "I don't expect to find anything, but can we head over to the campsite?"

We follow Raf out the door and experience the wall of heat again.

"Our car is over here. We can follow you."

"Leave it there. I'll drive."

Around the corner, Raf unlocks a black Ford F-250 four-door pickup with roll bar and a pair of high-powered spotlights mounted on the top. It sits at least a foot higher than stock and Gus has to pull himself up into the front passenger seat. I'm not exactly graceful climbing in the back seat.

I watch the controls for the air conditioner in front, waiting for Raf to turn the knob to high, when all four windows buzz down. I see the look of horror on Gus's face. He can't hide it and I almost laugh, if I weren't about to pass out.

"What can you tell me about the camp?" Gus says.

"Officers noticed the trailers pretty soon after they set up and checked them out to make sure they weren't squatting. It's an old airfield but the land is privately owned now. About ten years ago a developer picked it up thinking he'd turn it into a mall, but nothing ever came of it."

"They ever cause any problems?" I yell from the back seat to be heard over the wind noise.

Raf shakes his head. "They had a bonfire most nights so we got a few complaints about fire risk from over-concerned citizens. They had some guns, but everybody here does. Just like in Texas, right?"

"Yup. Just like Texas," Gus says.

I think Gus has become a part of the black leather seat. There may be a loud ripping sound when he tries to remove his skin from the material when we get out.

Raf turns off a secondary street onto a small road littered with potholes. Another quarter mile down, he comes to a stop.

Ahead of us is nothing. Just a big dirty brown field. Once we get out and start walking, I can see the remnants of the single runway. Marker lines are long worn off from the wind, dirt, and sand eroding away the paint. Turning to look back the direction we came from, the city of Yuma is not visible, the buildings all low to the ground and blending in with the brown surroundings.

"Good place to hide," I say.

"For being so close to the city you're pretty hidden here," Raf agrees. "Still, it's a tight community. We knew about them maybe a day or two after they settled in here."

"What was this place?" I say.

"This was Dateland. In World War II it was built by the Air Force. It was sold off a long time ago. At one point a developer was planning a large fly-in community. Houses lining the runway so you can land and pull right up to your house."

"That never happened?"

"Nah. Most people thought that it was crazy, and border patrol wasn't thrilled with the idea of more than four hundred houses with private planes so close to the border."

"Where's the border?" Gus says.

Raf turns and points. "About nine miles that way."

Gus and I turn to look south with him. The only thing visible is more brown.

Raf points to the west, across the border. "Over that way is Morelos. My family lives there. My grandparents were from Jalisco, down south, but moved to get closer to the United States so their kids could try to work on the other side of the border."

When we think of living in Texas, the border is a part of our history, our state's personality. The farther south in the state you go, the more immigrants you see who have made the move across the Rio Grande.

"Were you born there?" I ask.

Raf shakes his head. "When my mother was in labor, she walked across the border legally straight to the closest hospital. I was born three hours later. The next morning, still exhausted from giving birth, she called an immigration attorney in Yuma and never went back across again until she had her green card."

"And being a cop?" Gus lets the question ask itself.

"It was always important to me. As a boy growing up here, I saw how my people were mistreated. Police arrested you just for being brown. I wanted to be part of the solution."

"And is it better?"

"Most days."

We walk the area and Raf points out where the trailers had been parked. In the months since they'd left, any sign of them was long blown away, hidden by the dirt that covers everything else.

On the drive back to the city, Raf rolls the windows up and sets the air conditioner at 78, but it was still a relief.

"What are you two doing for dinner?"

"You have a recommendation for something authentic?" My mouth is watering at the thought of a real Mexican restaurant so close to the border.

"I have the perfect place." Raf pulls into his assigned parking space outside the police department. "Let me take you. I'll pick you up at seven."

"You really don't have to," Gus says.

"I insist."

CHAPTER 14

I blast the air in my hotel room at full speed, set to 66 degrees, for the two hours between checking in and Raf picking us up. It backfires on me, making the transition to the outside world even worse. My goose-bumped skin shrivels back into itself as soon as I open the door when Gus knocks.

"Raf's here." Gus is already sweaty.

The pickup is idling and the windows are rolled up when we reach the covered area outside the front door of the hotel, which makes me happy knowing that means the air conditioner is on. Gus climbs up into the front seat again and I get in back behind him.

He heads west from Yuma and we are on small dirt roads with wide open fields around us. The flatness is mesmerizing. After twenty minutes he turns onto a trail in a field and we carry on for several miles until we reach a barbed wire fence. Raf gets out and opens a gate, pulls the truck through, then closes the gate again.

The landscape hasn't changed. It looks no different than it had on the other side of the fence. Another mile and he pulls out of the field onto a worn out road.

"Raf," I say from the backseat. "Are we in Mexico?"

"Yes, we are," he says.

I see Gus tense up in the passenger seat.

"But we didn't pass through a checkpoint," I say. "We don't even have our passports."

"You have your FBI creds?" Raf says.

"Always."

"If anything happens, you'll be fine. But nothing is going to happen," he says.

I know what Gus is thinking. He just illegally crossed into Mexico. He's always been a by-the-book agent. Proper documentation. Detailed reports. A few years ago we ended up south of the border on a case. Though we went into Mexico through a checkpoint, we returned on a private airplane with the transponder turned off. It had been a life-or-death situation for a witness who was also a murder suspect. It was complicated. He still complains about being put in that situation. Now we just drove through a field into Mexico to have dinner.

"So I guess this will be pretty damn authentic food, then." I say.

"*Si*, yes." Raf takes a right turn in the huge pickup on the narrow road, causing three cars to back up to allow us to make the turn. The drivers all wave as if they know him. "The most authentic family style Mexican food you will find."

It's another fifteen minutes and the rows of buildings have faded to open fields. Raf turns down a dirt lane and the ground ahead of us lights up after he pushes a button to turn on the high-powered beams on the roll bar. It isn't too different from west Texas but still feels like another world. The glow of the lights show the rutted road we glide over, barely feeling the bumps with the aftermarket suspension on the truck.

He comes to a stop in front of a stone fence. Several other cars are parked outside. We walk through a small arched gateway and I don't know how he didn't brush the sides of the arch with his arms. A long, low-slung stone house with a terracota roof is set back with a large yard full of fruit trees between us and the front door. I wonder how he can even fit inside of the small structure, but instead of going through the door, we walk through the gate then around the side of the house.

"This doesn't look like a restaurant," Gus says.

"It is not."

"I'm guessing this is your family's house," I say.

"It is. They are expecting us, and are very excited to meet you both."

We come around the end of the home. String lights run everywhere above in various hues of incandescent glowing. The smell of meat over an open flame enters my nose and almost brings me to my knees, just then realizing how hungry I am. My last meal was take out from the Yuma airport when we landed. There are people everywhere talking, laughing, and dancing. A man older and larger than Raf who looks just like him is tending the grill.

"*Papá*." Raf hugs his father, then introduces us. "*Gustavo y Eddie*." He continues in his explanation of who we are and the only words I pick up are Austin, FBI, and important. I feel honored.

"*Hola, Gustavo y Eddie.*" That's the last thing I understood from his father. Raf translates our thanks to him.

We are taken through the large gathering and introduced over and over. Old Mexican women kiss us on the cheeks and small children orbit our legs everywhere we move. Tall, thick glasses are handed to us and we both sip. My eyes water immediately from the chili powder mixed with several juices and a healthy dose of tequila.

"What is this, Raf?"

"*Vampiro*," he says. "It is a traditional drink from Jalisco."

"It's amazing," Gus says.

"*Si*, yes." Raf raises his own glass to us then drinks it like water. "Most places outside Jalisco it is different, changed. Some places add tomato juice to the *sangrita*, the juices you mix with the tequila. But this . . . this is a proper *vampiro*."

I am suddenly very glad Raf drove, though he also has to get us back across the border, but something tells me he can handle quite a few *vampiros* before getting drunk.

The evening goes on into night with more incredible food than I thought was possible, and the drinks keep coming, but I never feel anything more than buzzed.

"It's the tequila," Raf says. "My family has their own label. Very high quality. It's only the other shitty stuff that makes you feel bad."

I watch Gus try to carry on conversations with several people, but the dialect is different and they talk too fast. He was born in Austin. His parents were born in San Antonio. He's never spent more than a few nights south of the border. For Austin, he's fluent in Spanish. In Mexico, he can't keep up.

CHAPTER 15

When I run, even if going through a case in my head, my mind is always analyzing threats around me. I'm not a paranoid man. It's just a way to stay sharp for the times there is actual danger. *Didn't that black SUV already pass me? Why's that guy wearing a hoodie in the heat?* There are always stories in police departments and even in the FBI of retired cops and agents getting mugged, or worse. They lost an edge they once had. They stopped looking at the world as law enforcement, and perhaps stopped carrying themselves like it, too.

I've never gone undercover. The movies get it wrong most of the time. Agents don't just go under. There are specially trained agents who devote their lives, their careers, to it. They move from city to city as needed to make sure locals don't know who they are. It's tough to go undercover when you were grocery shopping at Whole Foods in the same town every Sunday for the last ten years. I've rarely gone anywhere without my gun, or without Gus nearby. I'll be on my own and need to prepare. The landscape around the compound moves around my head and I begin my plan.

The heat cuts my run short. I keep waiting for the effects of the multiple *vampiros* from last night, but it never comes. Raf must be right about the good tequila. A cold shower to reduce the constant flow of sweat then I meet up with Gus at the rental car.

"Coffee?" Gus says.

"Hell no. It's already a hundred degrees at nine-thirty in the morning."

"I know what will feel good, then."

"Please don't say it like that."

"How about, I know what you want inside you?"

"Much worse."

He's driving us through Yuma as if he grew up here. I know his methods. He probably spent hours before we even flew out here studying the city map, and then some more this morning. Gus hates using navigation unless he needs to. Most cities are easy. They're grids. Figure out the numbering, and you're halfway there to driving like a local.

A few minutes later he pulls into a Sonic.

"I could kiss you," I say.

"Please do not."

"I said could, not will."

"Good. I don't want to explain that to Hope."

"Hey, what happens in Yuma …"

The large cherry limeades may not have the caffeine needed

to start the day, but they do have tons of ice to cool us down.

"What time is our flight?" I say.

"Two forty-five."

I glance at my watch. "Good. We can come back for more before we head home."

"As if we wouldn't?"

A short time later we walk through the Emergency Room doors at the first hospital on our list. Gus flashes his badge and a few minutes later we are talking to an E.R. doctor. We describe what we're looking for, the bruising and burns found on Buster Ballard and others. Nothing. Only a dozen other hospitals and clinics to stop at.

It's the seventh on the list before we get a hit, a smaller urgent care center that appears to cater to the uninsured and those not wanting to be entered into the electronic records system. Being this close to the Mexican border, it makes sense.

"It's been a while," the nurse says. "Probably a year."

"That sounds about right," Gus says. "You remember a name or anything else about him?"

"Average height. Average build." She looks me up and down. "About like you."

"I'm just average to you?"

She looks again. "Yeah."

"Ouch."

"I don't remember the name—been a long time, like I said. But I can try to go through my notes later and get back to you. It could take a while." She looks out at the people in the waiting area.

"I understand and really appreciate it," Gus says. He hands her a business card.

She stops us as we turn to go. "Did the others have the cuts, too?"

Gus and I look at each other, then at her.

"Cuts?" I say.

"Deep cuts. The M.E. said they were probably from a curved blade of some kind, and very sharp. Guy came in unconscious. We didn't even see the cuts at first, but when we moved him from the cot to the bed, blood started pouring out of them. He died on the table, so we never got any more information from him."

Back in the SUV, we sit with the air on full blast aimed right at our faces.

"Think we need to hit any more hospitals, or just knowing that there were similar victims here enough?" I say.

"I think we're good. Pretty much confirms it's the same group. Raf will contact us if he hears anything else."

"Back to Sonic, then?"

He glances at his watch. "Definitely."

On the flight home, Gus watches another movie and I rest my head, staring out the window and continuing to ponder my impending state of undercoverness. I'd be lying if I said I wasn't nervous.

We turn our phones on moments after the small plane touches down at Austin-Bergstrom and Gus's immediately buzzes with several messages.

"Got a name from the nurse in Yuma."

"That was fast."

"I'll run it in the morning. You go be with your girl."

"Same to you."

"I plan on it."

CHAPTER 16

"You remember the body out in Salt Creek?"

"You mean the dead guy we stopped to see on the way home from our vacation?" Eva says. "Yeah. I remember him."

"Right. There weren't any cuts on him, were there?" I say.

She lifts her eyes from the book she's reading, something by Barbara Kingsolver she's read at least a dozen times, and looks out the sliding glass door into the darkness for a moment.

"No." Her eyes are back to the book.

"Hmm." I settle back on the sofa and close my eyes to run what little we'd learned in Yuma around my head.

"What kind of cuts?"

I look up. Her book is closed on the floor beside her and she's turned to face me.

"What?"

"What kind of cuts?"

"Why?"

"It must be either important or something that doesn't fit or you wouldn't be thinking about it," she says.

She knows me. I tell her what the nurse said.

"Sounds like the cuts you came home with a while back," she says.

"What do you mean?"

"You don't remember? You woke up with our bed soaked in blood and said you didn't even know you'd been cut."

It feels like a cold draft of wind pushes around my body at the memory. It wasn't that long ago but I shoved it back into the pits with other bad things that have happened to me. It's hard to go into dangerous situations with the ghosts of every time you've been stabbed or shot hovering over you.

"The Nepali."

"Yeah. That's what you called him."

He had hit me twice with that curved blade weapon, a *Gurkha Kukri*. Clem had known what it was when I described it to him. It takes a warrior to know a warrior.

The whole case rushes back into my conscious thought as if I were still in the middle of it. Leocadia Ortiz, the former Army officer behind a rash of fuel thefts in Afghanistan, had carried her illegal activities into the civilian world. Her final moments in life were in a pickup rolling out of control down a rocky hill with us fighting each other in the front. My misfired bullet ended her. The Nepali had worked with her.

The darkness of my dream, the hooded figure. *Ruby rising.* It was him. That final time I saw him. It was outside my bar in the middle of the night. He'd appeared from nowhere and returned to it when he was done with his warning to me. A warning that hadn't made any sense at the time. His threat to not come for his true master, the ruby rising in the east.

CHAPTER 17

"I'm not as quick as I used to be." I look down at the browning grass across my father's grave. The white stone marker is dusty. I brush it off with my hands.

For the last several years of his life, my father had been a silent listener. Any thoughts or suggestions were lost inside the haze of his mind, unable to leave his mouth. I would sit beside him in the nursing home and tell him what was going on. Leaving the bureau. Meeting Eva. Injuries and cases that felt like I would never heal from. His silence had been my sounding board. He was a therapist who only listened, never offering any feedback. Occasionally there was the twitch of a hand or a gaze into my eyes that lasted for more than a few seconds and made me think there was something of him left inside the shell. His caregivers said he was in there. That he heard me, just couldn't respond. I like to think he wasn't. That is a hell I wish on no one.

Growing up the son of an Army man wasn't always easy. He was as cold and distant to my sister and me as he was to the soldiers under his command. Much of what I learned from him was in my efforts to not be like him. It pulled Shelley and me closer together, only having each other, especially after our mother died when we were still teens. We finished raising each other, which meant power struggles and fights, but in the end we prevailed. She's a mom and wife, and a successful paralegal, now back in classes to get her law degree in her late thirties. All of that keeps me from seeing her as often as I used to. We exchange occasional texts. Quick, bite-sized notes of encouragement and swear words to each other.

The cemetery is quiet as I sit down and lean on his stone, a closer embrace from him than I was ever used to. I can imagine him, six feet down, trying to pull away from the physical contact. The rumble of a louder than necessary exhaust goes by and I look over at the newer Mustang. A man younger than I gets out and takes a small bouquet of flowers and a fifth of Jack out of the back seat and walks to a grave a few rows over. He's wearing a tight white T-shirt with ARMY across the front. Tattoos peak out from under the sleeves on his thick biceps.

I look away when he sees me watching him, and I pull the phone from my pocket and tap out a message to Gus. A quick response comes back from him.

I'll talk to my SAC. We'll figure something out.

I think of the Nepali. He had been put out of mind and into the abyss of past attacks and injuries I choose not to dwell on. If ever there were a foe I hoped never to see again, he is one. The cuts alone aren't enough to make me think he's back and somehow involved in this. It certainly isn't his style, a militia in the middle of nowhere. His words about his true master, the ruby rising in the east, though. That has me worried.

CHAPTER 18

The two-decade old Toyota Corolla has no air conditioner, no stereo, and apparently no shocks as I bounce wildly over every bump in the highway. The back of the car is covered in contradictory faded stickers promoting everything from coexisting to pro-life, as well as many marijuana related images and one stating the old cliche, "You can take my gun when you pry it from my cold, dead hands." I don't know who had owned this car or what series of owners perhaps had culminated in this odd assortment of self-adhesive ideologies, but I figure there is something for everyone on there to keep from pissing any one single person off.

The odor emanating from the worn grey cloth upholstery can be best described as aged cigarette smoke and body odor. I keep the windows down. It doesn't help.

In the backseat is an old Army duffle bag donated by

Clem for the mission. It has seen plenty of wear and miles to not look like I'd just bought it at Urban Outfitters like a teenager trying to be ironic.

Eva was still asleep when Gus picked me up early yesterday morning. She may have woken up and stayed silent for all I know. She hates when I leave and, even more, she knows I hate leaving and having to say goodbye to her all over again after the night before.

My departure to the plains wasn't immediate. First I had to go to Gus's office to meet with the SAC for last minute instructions. Then I had to get semi-permanent tattoos applied to my skin. They go beyond the temporary ones you can order online, lasting weeks or even months if cared for. I'd watched in the mirror as a swastika was placed over my left pectoral muscle and several other variations on the theme on my arms and the back of my neck. Gus stood in the back of the room watching. He was more serious than usual. Seeing the symbols of hatred put on my skin was unnerving for both of us.

I couldn't even sleep my last night at home. I listened to Eva's breathing and stared at the ceiling thinking of every way this could go pear shaped. Gus and I have plenty of stories about going into a situation with no idea what to expect, but those were houses or buildings that might have armed baddies inside. Quick actions to gain advantage. We were out in minutes. This was days, a week, or weeks. We have no idea.

Gus will be near, sure. But not beside me. I'll have no way to call him or send a distress signal. I won't have a gun.

On one of my missions to Afghanistan with the Joint

Terrorism Task Force, I helped plan a mission for a team of Army Rangers into the mountains to get surveillance on what we thought was a terrorist cell. It was supposed to be two days. Out one night, back in camp forty-eight hours later. The drop from a C-130 in a HALO jump (a high-altitude, low-opening approach) meant to hide you from your targets. Before the first Ranger was on the ground, we knew something was wrong. Communication went dead from the team leader mid-air. He was supposed to confirm a safe landing after regrouping with his team, but it never came. We sat back at base for four days and nights, not knowing what happened to them. Airplanes took images and satellite imagery was gone over pixel by pixel, but there was no sign of them.

On the fourth night they drove back into camp in a stolen Toyota Hilux pickup that had more bullet holes in it than we could count. They were all there. One had a broken leg. All of them were exhausted and starving. Turned out our intel had been correct, but we were wrong about their location. Mid-air the leader identified the risk. They were descending right over the top of the terrorist cell. The radio was abandoned in fear it would be overheard or intercepted. Even a chirp of static interference on the enemies' radio could have alerted them to the Rangers' presence. The leader was able to get new non-verbal commands to his men and they redirected in freefall, landing less than half a mile from the enemy camp. That's where the one Ranger broke his leg on impact.

The next three days were spent hiding and trying to find a way out without being seen. The third night, a guard from the camp was walking right toward them and saw the sun's reflection off the sniper's scope. That enemy guard died less than a second after his revelation, but the damage was done. Two dozen men with AK-47s heard the crack of the sniper rifle and knew the Rangers were there.

When they rolled back into base, they had the leader of the terrorist cell bound and gagged in the bed of a stolen pickup. That's how Rangers do it. They don't stop. And that's how Gus and I are when we're together.

After I'd received my fake ink, Gus and I had spent the rest of the day sitting outside and talking. We never mentioned the mission. We were as prepared as we could be. It was time to decompress before recompressing, before becoming a tightly wound spring on the inside while trying to project something completely different to the group of well-armed cult or militia members I was to infiltrate. Last night I slept alone in a cheap motel near Lake Travis. I needed to look dirty and be dirty. No shower before leaving. No deodorant. I needed the musk of a man with no money and only the faintest hint of a plan. I needed to appear at the point of desperation, hungry and tired. That's what groups like this one look for. The weak.

The temperature seemed to climb with each mile driven farther from Austin, from my Eva.

I went through my approach plan in my head as a distraction from the road and lack of stereo. There were two items beside my duffle bag I had to prepare and drop off. My insurance policies. My escape plan, perhaps. Whatever they are, they are my emergency provisions. In one, a desert brown Glock 17 from the San Antonio field office. In the other, an untraceable satellite phone.

Several times I almost told Gus about my talk with Eva and the coincidences of the Nepali. His curved blade cutting deep and clean. His final words to me, *The ruby rising in the east.* But I don't. Because I don't want it to be true.

Occasionally I catch wind of my own armpits and have to turn away. I'm undercover now.

CHAPTER 19

There isn't enough traffic in Salt Creek for anyone to notice me sitting in the car across the street and a half block down from the one bar in town. Even if anyone had noticed, I don't think they would have cared.

We planned my arrival for Wednesday, the same day of the week I'd been here with Gus and had seen the crew from the camp show up. It was an educated guess. Perhaps they come every night, perhaps just Wednesdays. Maybe they hardly ever do and that had been a chance encounter.

I want a shower. Badly. It's been three days now since I've felt the cleansing spray of my large walk-in at home. Since then I've been tattooed with hate speech, dressed in clothes that looked like rejects from the Goodwill trash dumpster, and have walked through the dirt encrusted landscape to hide my emergency equipment. I think the car seats smell better than I do by now.

After two hours of stewing in my own stench in the Corolla, the red pickup passes me, headed toward the bar. I slouch down in my seat to avoid being spotted. The other pickup shows up a minute later. I watch from my rearview mirror. Six men total climb from the trucks. They are already loud and possibly drunk.

Fifteen minutes later I walk in the front door, shoulders rolled forward, hands in my jeans pockets, doing my best to look rejected by society, and sit at the bar. The six men are at the pool table. Their conversation is louder than the shitty bro-country music coming from the DVD jukebox, and that's the first thing I'm thankful for on the trip.

"Whaddya want?" The bartender leans his hands on the bar and looks at me.

"You got food?"

He looks me over, sizing up whether I have any money, then places a half-page piece of paper with maybe five menu items that looked like they were typed in 1974.

"Can I get the burger and some fries?" I say. "And a beer."

"We don't run tabs," the bartender said. "Be thirteen dollars. Plus tip."

I pull a wadded up ball of cash from my pocket. It was only sixty-three dollars. Enough, we thought, to get me some food and gas without looking like I had any real money to my name. I push two fives and five ones across the bar to him.

Without turning toward them, I put my attention on the men at the pool table. I can see them in the dirty mirror behind the bar. Though loud, they aren't saying anything more than insulting each other's pool playing and joking about how ugly their girlfriends would be if they actually had any. It was not informative at all.

When the paper plate with the burger and fries is dropped on the counter in front of me, I question all of my life choices in a single moment. Whatever I have done to bring me to this, sitting covered in filth in a west Texas dive bar with a hamburger in front of me that resembles a shriveled up and burned cow pie more than it does a piece of meat, is proof there is no god, or if there is, she hates me.

I take a swig of the beer and brace myself for the first bite. The bartender is across from me, prepared to judge my reaction. In my mind it's a test for an outsider. Another drink of beer to consider my options. Am I supposed to eat it or throw it on the floor?

With half my glass emptied, and knowing I will need the remainder of the cheap gold liquid to wash down the food, I choose my fate and pick the burger up. The bun crunches as my fingers push through the hard surface. I take a bite. While not good by any definition, it is far from the nightmare I'd prepared myself for. The bartender pushes off from the back of the bar and walks away. I have proven myself worthy.

My stomach strengthened from the battle of ingesting the burger, I move on to my mission. There has been no talking that offered any usable information to gain favor, so I go in hot.

I walk across the bar while pulling four quarters from my pocket. I place them on the edge of the pool table as the six men stop talking and look me over.

"I'll take the winner," I say.

The man who seems most like a leader in the group reaches over, picks up my quarters, and drops them in his pocket.

"I don't think so, buddy."

I look over at him. He has six inches on me and is wiry. His stained Marlboro T-shirt is a medium at best and still hangs on his frame.

"I just wanna play some pool and drink some beer," I say. "With you guys or without you."

I pull my last four quarters from my pocket and put them on the pool table. "Next game."

Again he reaches for the coins. As his hand opens to scoop them up, I drop my hand on top of his and push it down onto the edge of the table.

"With you or without you," I say again.

The man looks down at me as his eyes narrow. His stance doesn't change. Fists don't form. He doesn't pull away from under my hand. Then he looks past me.

I hear the step of a work boot fall behind me and duck as the wild swinging sucker punch toward the side of my head is thrown, and feel it brush across my hair, which is not long by any means. Too close. It was a right hook so I turn and bring my right elbow back into the ribs of the attacker, still in momentum forward from his strike, and feel a crack. It's hard to fight with a broken rib. Six men becomes five.

I rotate left and work around the table clockwise to only face off with one at a time, trying to disable each enough to keep them from wanting a second try, but without seriously injuring them. I don't need to send any to the hospital, just deter them from fighting and get their attention.

The next man lunges at me as I step over Broken Rib. His right jab goes wide and I bob and watch his left travel where my face should have been. Grabbing his left hand with my right, my other arm comes around him and flattens him onto the edge of the pool table. I slam his left hand down onto the stained green felt covered slate and feel a crack. Five becomes four.

As Cracked Hand screams in pain, I step into the approach of the next one to close the distance. He goes for the double-handed chest grab as if I had lapels he could grip, which I don't. His hands barely catch my T-shirt and I don't give him time to let go and rethink his strategy. My right hand goes over the top and grabs his far arm as my left comes underneath to catch his other elbow. With a twist I plant his face onto the hard slate table, and rotate his right arm backwards against the socket until I feel the pop I know well from having my own shoulder dislocated too many times to count. Four becomes three.

The next guy is stepping back as I come toward him, not giving the rest of them the luxury of being the attacker. His hands comes up, palms toward me.

"Stop, please," he says.

I glance over at the presumed leader who looks none too happy with his man, but also not thrilled about being outnumbered by one person. I go for the two-point conversion. I step past the man's outreached signal for peace, one hand goes to his neck, the other his belt buckle, and use him as a battering-ram to push into the guy behind him and send them into the pool cue rack on the wall.

I walk around the end of the table and stand face-to-face with their leader.

"Next game," I say.

He stares at me as the other men are climbing up off the floor.

"You can fight," he says.

I look at the broken gang, the blood stain on the pool table, and pool cues all over the floor.

"Or maybe they can't," I say.

"Haven't seen you here before. Where you from?"

"Are you a census taker?" I say. "Is it that time again already?"

He pulls the front of his shirt up to show the worn grip of an M1911 in the front of his jeans.

"That a .45 or are you just happy to see me?"

"I think it's time for you to go."

I pick up my four quarters and turn to leave, then stop. I reach my hand out to him, palm up. He doesn't look down at it and locks eyes with me until I see the slightest smirk. He pulls the other four quarters from his pocket and puts them in my hand. If I'm right, he figures he'll get them back soon enough.

CHAPTER 20

The town is so quiet I can hear the buzz from the one traffic light a block away. There's a slight click as it goes from red to green though no cars are waiting. I like small towns, but this one doesn't feel right. It has spent a hundred years fighting the elements and lost long ago but nobody has told the people who live here. At some point the streets were busier with workers from nearby oil fields and their families. A bank and a laundromat appeared. A café that probably served large stacks of pancakes with real maple syrup. The long worn and faded paint from the Duke & Ayres five-and-dime sits at the corner by the stoplight. The paper hanging in the windows has all fallen to reveal the empty blackness of the store, just like all the other businesses in town except the one bar that feeds, and feeds on, the locals.

My motel room is on the first floor facing the parking lot

as I requested. My Corolla is the only car. Salt Creek doesn't get a lot of tourists. The office is dark and locked as I walk by to fill my ice bucket to chill the two beers I have in my duffle. My last luxuries for a while.

I pause on my way back to the room and down the street at the town. The few streetlights aren't enough to block out the stars like back home in Austin. It's disorienting looking up at the dots of light. Eva and I had sat on the beach after dark a few weeks ago and stared at the constellations. Her hand found its way to mine and we let the sky be our entertainment. She deserves more of that, and views from better places than South Padre Island. Italy, maybe. Spain would be nice.

She asked me after my last big case if I ever considered retiring, from the detective work at least. I have the bar which could take more of my time if I wanted. Grow it, make it more successful than it already is. Austin is good to live music venues. I'd told her I think about it every time I'm sitting in a parked car watching a closed door across the street or pulling my weapon to defend myself. I can't stay faster than the other guy forever, and one of these days, he will best me, whomever he may be.

The lights over the room doors are off on my way back and I'm certain they were on when I walked out a few minutes ago. As I get to my door and pull my key out, I hear the dull tapping of an engine idling. The unmistakable drone of an older American V8. I see the faint glow of orange parking lights from around the corner of the building. Amateurs.

I figured they'd come, but didn't think it would be this soon. I thought I'd at least be able to have a decent beer first to help dull the eventual pain I'll be feeling.

I wonder for a moment if this is the day that the other guy will be faster, then I push it out of my head. Self doubt is the quickest path to death.

I turn the key and push the room door open. My lights are out and before it can register that I know I left them on, what is likely a baseball bat hits me in the gut. As I drop to my knees, a cloth bag is pulled over my head. The chemical smell isn't cleaning supplies. It's chloroform. Only problem is that unlike in the movies, it isn't instant. In this case it's a problem for me since while they wait for several minutes for me to pass out, I have to struggle to make it seem like they really surprised me, which means they are holding my legs down and punching me in the sides and back.

CHAPTER 21

". . . the bag off."

The words start to come through. My head doesn't feel like it's in a vice. It feels like a vice was thrown on top of my head then run over with a bulldozer.

I wince as the bag is pulled off, expecting bright lights to blind me, an attempt to disorient me further, a standard interrogation or torture practice. But it's still dark. I'm pushed to my knees, hands already tied behind my back. I feel the roughness of the soil. The bag that had been over me is on the ground. They had only been partially prepared. Someone thought to bring the chloroform but didn't bring a towel or bag, instead soaking the pillowcase from my motel room. I'll probably get charged for that.

A pointed cowboy boot lands firmly in the same spot on my gut the baseball bat had hit. What little beer and burger left in me sprays out through my mouth and nose, leaving that burning empty smell. I try not to fall forward into my own vomit.

"Who the hell are you?" I recognize the voice of the tall wiry man. He's in front of me so he wasn't the one who kicked. He's above that probably. Back at the bar he told his men to attack me without a word spoken. I know defeating him will get me nowhere but beaten up worse by those who listen to him. I must take out his men or befriend him.

"Eddie." I spit out more residue and taste some blood mixed with it.

"Eddie what."

Smart ass comments will only lead to more pain, and though it gives them all of the power, I give in.

"Eddie Green," I say. Just because I'm giving in doesn't mean I'll give them my real name.

Gus and I had spent two days creating Eddie Green. Using your own first name is smart when possible. It eliminates the chance of not paying attention to someone calling you by a different name because you aren't used to it. Eddie Green did six months in the Army before being dishonorably discharged for assaulting his drill sergeant. There were a few short stays in lockup since then for petty theft. Nothing that would have him jailed for long periods of time. He was from El Paso but has lived in San Antonio since getting kicked out of the military. We put enough out there in law enforcement systems to fool cursory glances, but further digging would find my pseudonym didn't exist before five years ago.

"What are you doing here, Eddie Green?"

"I just wanted to play pool."

I know the kick is coming and brace myself. The point of the boot luckily misses so I get the dull edge of a shin instead. I count it as a win.

"I'm gonna ask one more time. Your answer decides if you get to stand up and walk out of here or if your body gets to rot in the desert for the coyotes to chew on."

"Okay, okay," I say. I shrug my shoulder to get the hands from behind off me. The man nods and I'm released. Power. "Met a guy at a shelter a while back. He told me about a place out here he was headin' to."

"What guy?"

"Only got a first name. Buster. Only remember it because it's my cousin's name." I see a couple of the guys look at each other.

"What did this Buster guy look like?"

"Fuck, I don't know. Just another homeless guy looking for somewhere to go," I say. "Looked like me. Looked like you. He had ink like mine. Only reason we ever talked."

The man nods again and my shirt is pulled up to reveal the swastikas and the other images and words of white supremacy.

"You think just because of that you can walk right in and beat the shit out of my guys?"

"No. Like I said. I wanted to play some fucking pool with you, you sack of shit. You're the one who had your team of thugs attack me. I just defended myself. I was hoping you knew Buster."

Some whispers and stifled laughs behind me.

"Shut up," the man says over my head and it falls silent

again. "Where'd you learn to fight like that?"

"A dad that beat me and three older brothers who took after our dad. What the fuck does it matter to you?"

"Skills like that come in handy where we live," he says.

"Well, you haven't seen anything yet."

"I get the feeling you're right."

Another nod and I'm kicked in the gut again and pushed face down on the ground. In pain and my hands tied behind me I still know I could take them, even from this position. That's not egotistical, just fact. I'd fought most of them already, if you can call it a fight. But there's four more of them. I let myself relax in the dirt, a size eleven boot on my back. The pillowcase is picked up and placed over my mouth and nose. The chloroform has faded but is enough to take my will to fight away. I'll beat them up later.

CHAPTER 22

I wake up in the dirt. A rattlesnake is shaking its tail not far from me, fangs exposed. I'd rather take on the six men in a bar fight again. My arms and legs are heavy from the last weak dosing of chemicals, but I need to move slowly anyway, so I work my way backwards from the snake, never taking my eyes off it.

It looks about three-feet long. Not huge, but big enough to do damage. Gus was the Boy Scout, but I've picked up enough outdoors knowledge over the years. I keep moving slowly until I'm five feet away. A rattler can strike from two thirds of its body length, so I was out of range from a strike, but the damn thing can move fast if it decides to uncoil and come after me.

On my feet, I back farther away, keeping an eye for any more snakes so I don't step on one. I'm finally able to look around more than the immediate ground in front of me. I turn and see the outlines of the trailers and fence of the camp a half mile away. They'd left it to be my choice, I guess. I'd proven myself enough to walk away if I wanted, or to try reaching them again. That's a tactic cults use. Let people choose for themselves, or let them think they are choosing for themselves. It gives the leaders more power over them than being taken by force. A member who wants to be there is moldable. Teachable. One who is abducted only wants escape, at least until they are broken.

I start toward the camp. The sun is barely up and I see the other nocturnal creatures running for final prey before retreating for the hot day. A pair of coyote stop and stare at me from no more than thirty feet away before continuing on.

My body stiff, it takes longer than it should to reach the camp. When I do, the gate is already slid open. No pickups are blocking the way. A man is on each corner with an assault rifle hung low on his back. Nobody waves or invites me in, but they don't stop me, either.

I walk into the camp. In the middle is the smoldering remains of the big bonfire Gus and I had seen. A clattering noise behind me as the gate slides closed. There's no welcoming committee or goody bags waiting. I'd kill for some fresh baked chocolate chip cookies like at one of the many open houses Eva and I visit for fun on days off just to see other homes in the area and eat free cookies. It's a simple pleasure.

There are three small houses made of cinderblock bases and wooden walls. Small black metal chimney pipes come out of the roofs. Two trailers form an L to the houses. Both have tires and look like they may have made the trip from the Yuma camp. Past the far house I see the back end of my sticker-covered Corolla. My duffle bag is on the trunk. I never even got to drink my beers.

The door to one of the small houses opens and the tall man from last night comes out. He's dressed in the same clothes but has a cowboy hat on now. If you'd have asked me last night if he could get away with wearing a cowboy hat, I'd have said no. But now that I see him, he makes it work.

As he approaches me, doors to the houses and trailers open. Men come out and stand beside their dwellings. I recognize the other five men from last night.

"You don't give up, Eddie Green," the man says.

"I like to punish myself," I say.

"Everyone needs a hobby, I guess," he says.

"You know my name, but I have no idea who you are."

He looks around at the men standing beside the buildings and trailers.

"We don't have names anymore," he says. "There is no need for them here."

"Doesn't that get confusing when the mail comes?"

For a moment he looks like he tasted a lime. He's not a fan of my humor.

"These men are all here because they want to be, and they proved themselves worthy, as did I," he says. "Nobody uses names, but two have titles. I am The Second. And we all serve the Ruby."

"I see, Mr. The Second. Is Buster here or isn't he?"

"Your jokes are tiring and unnecessary, Mr. Green." He walks toward me. "If you wish to stay with us, you will learn that they are no benefit to you. Your friend you call Buster, he is no longer here. He served his time and moved on to the next level."

"The next level?"

He nods. "Yes. We are a family, you could say. But closer than brothers. We have no secrets from each other. Nothing any of us has done before arriving here matters, only what we do now. We keep twelve men here. No more. No less."

"I only count eleven," I say.

"A servant moved on just two nights ago," The Second says. "Your arrival is either coincidence or conspiracy. I do not know which yet."

"I told you, was just looking for Buster and a place to stay. I'm not a bum. I earn my keep. You saw what I can do last night. But I can do more."

The Second walks in silence, the shade of his dark brown cowboy hat in the midmorning sun shielding his eyes. He doesn't look at me or the other men, just circles the remains of the fire, then stops and turns to me.

"You still have your name, Mr. Green. The anonymity of those that serve the Ruby is earned."

"How is that done?" I don't want to seem too eager, but also don't want to be out here trying for weeks. I decide to be easily indoctrinated.

The Second smiles. "Three tasks are to be completed. To be considered for the tasks, one must walk through the gate on their own. You have done this, of your own free will."

I decide not to point out that they had in fact stolen my

car and possessions and have them here. Instead I try to act as if I'd just made my daddy proud and stand a little taller.

"From there, if I deem the visitor worthy, the next task can commence."

"What's the next task?"

"You must relinquish all of your possessions and offer them to the Ruby."

"You already have my car and bag," I say. "There's not much in the duffle and to be completely honest, I stole the car in Austin last week. But it's all yours. Or, the Ruby's, I guess."

"Your gift is received. Once everything has been inspected and evaluated, your clothing will be returned to you. It is the offering of the gift that shows your value. The Ruby thanks you."

"What's the final task?"

"This is what brings a dilemma," he says. "One we have never encountered before. I met with the Ruby at sunrise to inform him in case you did choose to walk through the gate. He was skeptical but I described your abilities and he was impressed. You see, the final task is that of physical valor. A fight. Men are chosen from our ranks and you must remain standing."

"Sounds like I did that last night," I say.

"Which is exactly what I explained to the Ruby. He was reluctant to accept those events as you were not performing with knowledge of the task. The Ruby is wise and pointed out that fighting in a bar to defend yourself and fighting a brother for nothing more than victory are not equal. You must fight for the Ruby, not yourself."

"So I have to fight again?"
"You do."
"When?"
"Tonight."
"Sounds fun."

CHAPTER 23

One of the men leads me to the trailer on the end. It's the smallest and looks as if it has been through a few tornados. Inside the thin metal door the smell hits me. I gag and am glad I have no food in my stomach to lose.

"Over there," the man says.

In the back corner beside the broken door to the bathroom is a thin cot mattress on the floor. There's no pillow, sheet, or blanket. I really am spoiled.

"Is there turn down service?" I say.

"What?"

"Nothing. This looks good." I don't want to put my body on that mattress. Maybe I can end all of this before bedtime.

Two others come in and stand between me and the door. One has a removable cast on his hand. The other has bandages around his ribs with his shirt hanging open.

"No hard feelings, guys. Right?" I say.

They don't respond. One grabs a deck of cards from his bag and they leave.

The man who had shown me to the trailer looks out the door after them.

"Don't let them bother you," he says. "Some of the guys don't take to people until they've been here a while."

"And after they've been here a while?"

"Well, usually they still don't like 'em. We all just wanna prove ourselves and move on to serve the Ruby."

"Who is this Ruby person?"

"He's the Ruby."

"Right, but how do you serve him? What's his deal? Do we chant and dance around a fire or sacrifice virgin bunnies for him?"

"Nothing like that. We do whatever he asks. This is like, you know, the front lines. We're the little guys," he says. "The ranch is where you wanna be."

"The ranch?"

"It's where the Ruby lives. He has his own people there that serve him. That's where you go when you leave here."

"Have you been there?"

"Once. Well, in a barn there."

"What for?"

He looks out the door again to make sure nobody is near. He's shorter than me, but stockier. A few scars on his face and his nose has definitely been broken at least once. I think he could hold his own for a few minutes in a fight. Along with the guys I took down at the bar, I don't have much to worry about in the final task.

"Not supposed to talk about it," he says. "You ain't passed the tasks yet."

"Ahh, right. I don't want to get anyone in trouble. Say, what do you all call each other since you don't have names?"

"We don't. Well, we try not to but it's just hard sometimes. Those two goons who came in are Larson and Jacobs. Don't know their first names."

"Did you know Buster Ballard?"

He looks up at me quickly.

"You seen Buster? He okay?"

"Not since before he came here. Was hoping to find him." No need to tell him Buster is dead.

A horn sounds from one of the pickups outside.

"Shit. I gotta go. My time on the fence."

"On the fence?"

"We rotate for security," he says. "Just in case the feds come, you know."

"The fed? Like FBI?" I say.

"FBI, ATF, CIA, any of those fuckers."

"Right. Wouldn't want that."

I have nothing to leave at my dirty mattress on the floor so I step out of the trailer and explore the compound while trying to keep from looking as if I'm exploring the compound. It's a rectangle with one of the short ends at the gravel road.

The compound fence is your normal chain link going up about fifteen feet with two strands of barbed wire forming circles along the top edge. Don't know if that's to keep people in or keep them out. I know it wouldn't slow the feds down any. The fence isn't dug into the dirt, so there's plenty of places it can be pulled up enough to shimmy under if you don't mind getting dirty and your tetanus shots are up to date. In the back corner I find a bit of shade from the side of a house and the end of a trailer with a view of most of the compound.

Standing near the burned wood I can feel heat still emanating from the ashes. A fire that large takes a long time to fully burn out, especially if not smothered with water. Soon, more wood will be added, and, knowing these fools, a gallon of gasoline will be poured over them to make sure it starts quickly. In the ashes I see pieces of metal cans that have exploded from the heat. In my mind I picture the fights that take place and feel my future getting closer.

CHAPTER 24

Just after dark we form a line beside the bonfire that now blazes a dozen feet into the air. Everyone is quiet. The usual nonstop banter and insults between the men is gone, replaced by solemn expressions. They seem to know something I don't. Shoulders are back and all eyes are on the gate. I'd like to say we are all showered and dressed nicely, but we aren't.

The day had been quiet. I sat in the shaded corner and kept to myself, which was easy since nobody wants to be near me. The tall man who calls himself the Second left after lunch and only returned a short time ago.

A murmur from the men, then reverent silence again as the headlights appear. Three vehicles pull in through the open gate, which is rolled closed behind them then padlocked so the guards can return to the fire. The first and third SUVs are black Cadillac Escalades. The windows are down and men sit sideways in the rear seat as I've seen countless Secret Service agents do when detailed to the highest offices in D.C. The middle vehicle is a bright red Range Rover.

Men get out of the Escalades in black V-neck shirts with black slacks and form a perimeter around the middle SUV. They each have black shoulder holsters with ridiculously large silver pistols hanging in them. From a distance they look like .50 caliber Desert Eagles, the least practical sidearm there is, whose only value is visual impact and a deafening boom. With eyes scanning, the rear door of the Range Rover is opened and a man steps out. He's wearing white slacks and jacket with a white T-shirt underneath that is losing the battle of controlling his expanding belly. If he had a white beard he'd be a dead ringer for Richard Attenborough in *Jurassic Park*.

I lean to the man beside me. "Is that the—"

"Shh."

I shh.

The Second greets the man I now presume to be the Ruby, all but curtsying to him. They are too far away to hear, especially over the growing crackle of the bonfire behind me. The men in line with me all stand a little taller at once when another figure comes out from around the red Range Rover. He's wearing black pants that are too baggy and a black hoodie up over his head. His gait and movements are controlled, almost effortless as he appears to glide more than walk. He stops behind and to the left of the Ruby.

My eyes don't leave the slight shadow of a man, already blending in to his surroundings as he seems to intend. His outline shimmers against the dark background, shades of black messing with my eyes. His raises his head and looks around for the first time. Within the darkness of the hood I can barely make out his face from the reflection of the fire behind me on his skin, and I know who he is.

I reach my hand to my side as a ghost pain burns momentarily. The blur of the hooded figure a year ago slipping past me, striking without any impact, or so I thought, until Eva discovered the blood seeping from my abdomen the next morning. The memory that has been taunting me for days now.

He is the Nepali.

And that last time I saw him, outside my bar late at night, he had talked about the ruby rising in the east and it made no sense. Now it all does—or some of it, at least. Okay, small parts. The man in the white suit had been behind everything a year ago. Behind Leocadia Ortiz and her crimes. That all may have gone undiscovered if it hadn't been for her greedy husband selling pot on the side.

This man is the Ruby. I had been warned by the hooded figure to not search for him, yet here I am. I wonder briefly about if I had even remembered his foreboding words on the sidewalk in downtown Austin and connected them immediately to the information about Ruby Rising, LLC, if I would not have allowed myself to be in this situation. And I know I would have.

The Ruby moves toward us with the Second beside him and the Nepali following. I find myself thinking fondly of when people had real names only a few days ago. I'd love to meet a Carl right now. Or a Jennifer. Simple names. They move down the line of dirty men who all smell from days or weeks without showers, sleeping in filthy trailers, and living in the dirt of the Texas plains. The Ruby looks at each man as he passes, then pauses in front of me, turning to face me straight on.

"You are the one to be tested." His voice is higher than I expected.

I didn't know if he was declaring it or asking.

"Yes?"

He looks me up and down and turns away with an unimpressed look then announces to the group, "Three." Then he walks away.

The men all start moving and talking. Most stay away from me, except for my nameless bunkmate.

"What was that all about?" I say.

"It's the trial. The test."

"Right. I get that. But what did he mean by three?"

"Oh, you have to fight three men to pass."

Out loud I say, "Three?" I want to feel confident about it. It is likely that one or all of them will be men I beat in the bar, but they may be more inspired this time to keep me from joining their ranks.

CHAPTER 25

The commotion settles after the announcement. I've been standing silently, running drills in my head to prepare. I eye each man, sizing him up based on our past experience, or if it's one I haven't scrapped with, how he moves and carries himself. You can tell a lot about how a man will fight by how he moves. The only one who carries himself like a fighter is the Second, and he is above the men and has likely earned his place to not fight anymore.

I stand alone by the fire. The other men are huddled up near the Second. I catch words here and there of them volunteering themselves to be one of the three or making excuses why they shouldn't be, mostly from a couple of them that I beat in the bar.

The Ruby gets out of his Range Rover again and saunters back toward the fire. Chairs have been set up for him and the Second. The Nepali stands behind them. The security force is spread out facing away from the fire, watching for the feds, I'm guessing. If they only knew.

The Second comes out to me and makes the pre-fight announcements and gives the rules. It turns out there really aren't any rules. Essentially the last man standing wins a fight.

"If a fighter is able to burn his opponent in the fire, that man is banished from the camp," the Second says. He turns toward the other men. "Will the selected three please step forward."

Three walk toward us. Only one was from the bar fight, and he is chosen to go first.

The Second turns to me and speaks softly. "Don't hurt them too badly."

All ceremony is dropped as the Second returns to his chair beside the Ruby. I look at the man facing me and hold my right fist out.

"What's that?"

"Tapping gloves," I say.

"We're not wearing gloves."

"I know. It's what you do. It's like saying have a good fight. It's showing respect for your opponent."

He looks even more confused. "Fuck that."

"Let's get this over with, then," I say.

As soon as I'd seen who my first fight was with I replayed the bar scene in my head. Each encounter was short, but I remembered every move with each fighter. This man had been fourth.

I look him in the eyes and when I see him ready to go I take a half step left, his fist passing just by my head as I recall he favors his right. His chest is exposed by committing the solid straight punch and misses. My right knee comes directly up into his gut, doubling him over. My right leg then comes around and over him and down on the back of his neck, sending him to the ground. He doesn't get up.

It was less than ten seconds.

The other men are silent before what seems like forced cheers come from them. The man is lifted up by his arms and dragged away, dirt and cigarette butts stuck to his sweaty face as he grunts in pain. I felt at least one rib break when my knee struck him.

The Second stands again and motions to the next fighter.

This one is taller and seems more athletic. He begins to throw punches in the air as either a way to warm up or an attempt to intimidate me, but since the air isn't punching him back, it doesn't work. From the shadowboxing, I notice the man's right arm has more pop to it and assume he is right arm dominant, and likely right leg dominant, if he even knows how to kick, that is.

The Second sits down. Once more I extend my fist and this man reaches out and taps it in the sign of respect between opponents. He moves back into fighting stance, left leg forward, confirming my assumption, so I step back with my left putting him at an immediate disadvantage to his power strikes. I consider trying to end it quickly like the first bout, but I fear if I take all three down too easily that the Second may just keep sending more at me, so I decide to make it last.

He comes in with a front leg hook kick, likely trying to get me to step back with my right to open my front up to his power kicks, but instead I stutter step back. I recognize his moves. Tae Kwon Do. It was the first style I studied before moving on to other practices. He brings a second hook kick. Instead of moving back this time, I bring my left leg up, tighten my body into a turn kick, and my foot lands in his exposed stomach while his hook glances off my back with no damage.

Even though I struck hard, he is back in stance quickly, unfazed. This one will be more fun than I expected.

We move around each other with punches and kicks, some landing, others glancing off. He gets a solid strike on my left cheek which I returned with a roundhouse to his chest while he was exposed.

He's good, there's no questioning that, but he's strict. Nothing strays from proper form and style, and so far I have done the same. He has probably competed before, perhaps at high school level karate tournaments. I can stick with Olympic style fighting, or change it up to throw him off, and have a little fun at the same time.

These men are here because it is the best place they can find, likely after getting out of jail or on the run avoiding being thrown in one. It's a half-step above being homeless. I don't want to hurt them, but I need to do my job.

I put a little more distance between us with each step as we move, so minutely it is hard to tell if it is him or me getting farther away. We are out of range for striking without advancing, and I wait. It is a few more steps in our orbiting that I see his hips adjust and I get ready.

He comes at me with a series of roundhouse kicks, Tae Kwon Do basics for closing distance. A right, a left, and then as he brings the right that he intends to knock me down with, I rotate with him and step back, putting the impact several inches past where his peak power is. My right arm grabs his leg at the shin and my left is at his right shoulder grabbing a handful of dirty flannel. We are face to face as my left leg comes around his and acts as the fulcrum, his body the load, and my momentum the force, as he is flung backward to the ground. The thud of his body on the dirt is audible.

He gets up slowly and I let him take his time. I can tell he is shaken and a bit winded, not used to being taken to the ground so easily. His next series of punches have a fraction of the force behind them and his kicks aren't much better. I let him land a couple of strikes then step around the next one, put his right arm in a lock as my left goes around his neck from behind and I bend him over backward until I am supporting his weight. Thirty seconds later he collapses from the temporary disruption of oxygen to his brain.

CHAPTER 26

There is less cheering.

The man is helped up after he comes to. The third fighter chosen steps forward, looking timid in doing so. I do my best not to grin.

The Second stands and steps between us. He looks at the rest of the men, then at the next fighter, and motions for him to move back into line.

"Impressive, Mr. Green," the Second says.

"Thank you."

He looks over at the Ruby, who offers the slightest nod possible, an approval to commence. For a moment I think the Nepali will come forward. I don't know if I'm ready for that. I catch his eyes beneath the black hood and can't tell if he has recognized me. Then the Second pulls his shirt off to reveal a toned and sinewy chest and arms, nothing like I expected. It wasn't the body of a weightlifter, but of a fighter, likely mixed martial arts.

"So, a change in the fight card?" I say.

"Yup."

"Is it to protect your men, or—"

"I want to see what you have," he says.

"Okay, then."

"And you're not going to hold back like you did with the others," he says.

"I wasn't—"

"You were."

"Yeah. I was."

We circle each other and for the first time I really notice his smoothness, his conciseness of motion. I mistook it for old school cowboy sauntering, but I was wrong.

I usually like to wait for my opponent to strike first, but I can tell he isn't going to. He's playing it very cool, reserved. I launch a tight right hook to his face, even though he has a good six inches on me, thinking it wouldn't be expected. He barely flinches and doesn't step back, only moves his head enough to let my fist fly past. I try again but follow the right hook with a straight left to the sternum but it never reaches its target. A flurry of punches land on my face and chest. They are powerful but not overpowered. Enough to let me know what I have in store.

He's right. I'm not going to hold back.

But the Second is a challenge. He has the movement and skill of someone who trained not in a karate school you pay monthly, but from a master that makes you carry buckets of water up a thousand stairs without spilling a drop or you have to start over again. There is a zen peacefulness to his fighting. A lack of reaction to being struck, strikes forgotten as soon as skin meets skin, what happened has happened and isn't to be dwelled on type of shit. It's hard to piss someone off when they don't react at all. An angry fighter is a sloppy fighter, and I'm not going to be able to make him angry.

We continue to work on each other, neither taking an advantage of more than a few strikes before the other takes control again. Adrenaline is in overdrive. I realize I won't beat him by going toe to toe, or even in a ground game. He took his shirt off not only to show me his strength, but to remove my ability to grab him and I didn't realize it early enough. If he decides to grapple, I'm in trouble. But also he can stand outside my strike zone and still reach me with his longer arms and legs, so maybe I need to get him in close.

I match him kick for kick and punch for punch for another series, then take a calculated risk and step behind his next roundhouse. My hands grab at his chest as I had done with the previous fighter but there is nothing but sweaty skin to hold onto. He knows that and brings his hand to my shirt and moves to throw me. In the fraction of a second before his leg can get into position to launch my body over it, my arms move through his, holding one hand to my chest and locking the other elbow. His arms flex as instincts kick in, knowing what I'm about to do, but it's too late. I drop back to my right knee, his body forced to follow in an awkward and off balance move forward, his height advantage now a deficit to him as I roll back, bringing the momentum of his weight forward above me, my left foot going into his groin to be the fulcrum this time. I release his hands to let him hit the ground so I can spin around on my hip to gain further advantage, but he grips my wrists in anticipation.

I use his hold and pull my legs up and in a gymnastic move my neck and shoulders will hate me for later, I flip over on top of him. His grip is gone and I land several punches in his face. He tries to land a strike to my side but has to keep protecting his face until he simply rolls over and pushes me off. Blood comes out of his mouth and left eye.

We both get up and circle again. For the first time I see a slowness in his step. My hits to his head took a toll. I don't give him time to recover and go in with a combination, starting with a roundhouse to close distance, a spin kick to drop his arms, and a lunging straight right punch to the chest to knock the wind out of him.

He stumbles then recovers. I move in again, beginning with punches to keep him confused, then a knee up into his abdomen. An uppercut once he's bent forward and he's moving backwards toward the fire with no control, arms still out in front of him, but his wind gone and his legs are about to come out from under him.

I jolt forward and grab his outstretched arms right before he falls into the fire. I pull him back and he comes forward with a final punch which I let land softly on my chest. My arm around him, I walk him back over to his men and they take him from me.

CHAPTER 27

Time moves slower in the desert, or so it seems. The men keep to themselves, or at least away from me. I don't see the Second again for two days. Within the confines of the fence there is little to do, and I doubt I'll get an invite to their weekly bar outing.

I've completed their three tasks. I want to move things along. Being undercover isn't as fun as the movies make it seem. I'd rather be sleeping in my own bed next to Eva instead of on a thin cot in a trailer.

Buster Ballard's body is in limbo somewhere in a Texas morgue and I'm not any closer to finding out what happened to him, aside from the obviousness of the fight and the fire. There is more to this group than I know yet.

Somehow the Ruby controlled Leocadia Ortiz. Did he own her before she was in the Army stealing fuel and selling it to the highest bidder, or did he find her after she was out and use her crimes as leverage to carry out his will, stealing and selling fentanyl and other opioids? I've seen no sign of drugs or drug use at the compound, so the product she was selling didn't make it here. I think to when the final bullet struck her, the hang fire that paused time, and to when the men here at the compound were recruited from an abandoned airfield in Yuma, Arizona. The men came after. A response to losing Ortiz and the drug trade, perhaps. A new group of men to carry out the illegal operations to support the Ruby. If he knew about her demise, did he know who I was? If not, the Nepali surely does.

The mood the night of the fights changed quickly after I defeated the Second. The men all disappeared to tend to him, and to stay away from me. I doubt he needed to go to the Emergency Room. The Ruby was back in his Range Rover without a word by the time I turned my attention away from my fight. The Nepali stood behind the red SUV. I couldn't see his eyes beneath the hood, but he was facing me. I don't know if he recognized me, but it has been two days and I'm still alive. I would have woken up with him above me as his curved blade ended me had he realized who I am. Or I just wouldn't have woken up at all.

I sit in the shaded corner where I can watch the movement around the camp. It doesn't take long to figure out their guard schedule or where they keep the assault rifles the guards carry. None of the men carry sidearms. A black SUV comes once a day and delivers food, which is attacked with the ferociousness of hyenas on a dead lion carcass. I take scraps that are left, avoiding getting too close to the others until they are ready to be close to me, if that ever happens. My first time undercover is going swimmingly.

Men leave at night. Not in the two pickups, but different vehicles that pick them up. The Second is always there as they go, but never accompanies them. When they return, he meets them at the gate again. This is an activity of the compound to which I am not privy to yet, what I can only guess is the fundraising component. The drugs or guns or whatever it is they are selling illegally.

In the quiet of the desert, the hum of the single air conditioner in the camp comes from the small building the Second lives in. I don't blame him for not coming out very often.

Thoughts turn easily to Eva and the comfort of her arms. I miss her. I think of where I'll take her when this is over. The Amalfi Coast, perhaps. Or the south of France. Anywhere with pleasant heat, nice beaches, and great food will do. She'd be happy with San Diego. Retirement is sounding better and I imagine what I would do with my days without cases to work and leads to follow.

It's the morning of the third day after the fights—Sunday, I think—when anyone speaks to me again. It's the same man who showed me where my bunk was.

"The Second wants to see you."

"He does?"

"Yeah. He does. Meet him at the main gate in ten minutes."

The Second is standing with his back to me as I approach the gate. It slides open when I reach him. He starts walking.

I follow. No words are spoken.

He has a long sleeve flannel shirt, unbuttoned, with a not-too-clean white T-shirt underneath. Thin work gloves are on his hands which may be to cover up bruises from the fight. I'm on his right as we walk through the gate. I think I see the smallest bulge of a holster on his hip. I think of all the gangster films I've watched that end like this. Your so-called hero led out to the desert or a clearing in the woods or the Jersey shoreline. They're pushed to their knees and a gun is put to their head. If that's what this is he'll need some backup to make me go without a fight.

I'm not known for my silence in most circles. Snarky remarks and sarcasm are my go-to conversation starters, and enders. But I read the room and stay reserved and quiet, instead concentrating on the ground ahead of us and watching for rattlesnakes. I also watch for cherry limeades, but am not hopeful as the desert isn't their native environment.

"Nobody's beaten me in a long time." We've walked at least a mile before he speaks.

"It wasn't easy." It isn't a lie.

"You're very good. Controlled. You fooled me with your fake grappling move. You may not have won if it weren't for that."

"I agree. You gave me the best challenge I've had in a long time and I needed an advantage."

"It was well seen and executed."

I'm in the desert with the second-in-command of some band of merry marauders or cultists or something who may have a pistol and a loss to avenge. It isn't my best day. I look around for reflections of binoculars that might be Gus watching from afar, but see none. I'm not concerned about other guys from the camp ambushing me. The Second isn't like that. If he has a grudge, he'll handle it himself.

He stops walking and I do a half step after.

"We can use you here," he says.

"For what?"

"You're a smart guy. I'm sure you've figured out a few things."

"Like the late night comings-and-goings?"

"Like that."

"I've seen them, yeah. Don't know what they are," I say.

"But you can guess."

"I can."

"Does it bother you?"

"I've done time."

"I know."

"Then you have your answer."

He nods. "You'll fit right in."

"Once the rest of the guys accept me."

"Don't worry about them. They're mostly a bunch of crybabies," the Second says. "We have a job in a couple of days. Are you ready?"

"Don't know what it is, but I'm ready to get it going, sure."

He nods and looks at the horizon, scanning with an intensity that now makes me hope Gus isn't out there watching, a glint off his binoculars giving him away and me by proxy.

"I know you're a good fighter," he says. "How are you with a gun?"

"I'm capable." I lie.

The Second pulls the flannel shirt back on his right hip to expose a worn brown holster. He takes the grip of the pistol and draws it. It's a cheap gun. Black and compact. He raises and aims at a scraggly tree that is struggling to survive out here even before the extra insult of being shot at. I watch his movements, ready to react if he turns on me, though it is doubtful after the conversation we've been having.

Three shots are fired. I miss my ear protection. I have fired my weapon too many times without it to flinch, but do anyway for show.

"Here. Give it a try." He flips the gun in his hand and holds the barrel with his gloved hand and offers it to me.

I look at it for a moment. "I'm really not that great with pistols. More of a rifle guy." I take the pistol and act uncomfortable with it.

I get a closer look. A Hi-Point C-9 9mm. Eight in the magazine and one in the chamber when fully loaded. If it were, then I have six shots remaining. Would he take that chance?

I raise and aim at the same tree, letting my left hand slide under my right instead of up in proper grip, and pull the trigger to fire one round. It misses the tree, sending dirt up a good ten yards past it.

The Second looks out to where my bullet hit and grins.

"At least you're good with your hands," he says.

I give him the gun and he places it back in the holster. The flannel shirt falls in place over it. We turn to walk back.

"Can you give me any information on the job?" I say.

"Soon," he says. "The Ruby will send me word and I'll let you know."

"What happens at the ranch?" I say. "One of the guys said that men can move there from the compound if they prove themselves."

"I wouldn't be worrying about that. You haven't even been on your first job yet."

The rest of the walk is quiet. As we reach the gate it slides open and lets us back in.

"Thank you for the walk," I say.

He removes his gloves and reaches his right hand out and gives me a firm handshake. His knuckles are red, but not bad.

"Thank you," he says.

CHAPTER 28

Two more long days in the desert watching and waiting while at the same time trying to not look like I'm watching or waiting. I pick up more names of the men as they talk to each other not thinking I can hear, or not caring if I can. The black SUVs bring food, then late on the second day bring something else. In a white rental van following the SUV are four cases of beer and a dozen bottles of Jack Daniels. There's also ten women who stumble out in varying states of impairment, from just plain drunk to high on crack.

The Second comes out of his building and watches as the beer and liquor is stacked up and the women are looking around, not sure of what is happening.

"Tonight is a night to relax, men," the Second says. "Drink, laugh, and fuck!"

With that the party begins. Beers are tossed around

and sprayed over each other and quickly consumed. The Jack Daniels is treated more respectfully, with plenty being offered to the women.

The Second works his way through the group, eyeing each woman, until it is obvious he has chosen one and she is taken back to his shelter. None of the men protest his choice, though several had already sidled up to her.

The math doesn't work out in anyone's favor. Twelve men and ten women. I can remove myself from that count, but still it is eleven to ten. Someone is sharing.

A hand slaps down on my shoulder as the strong stench of whisky hits my face.

"Better pick you one before they're gone, new guy." It's my bunkmate, the guy who showed me around that first day.

"I'm good," I say.

"There's enough to go around," he says. "I'll even team up with ya on one of 'em. You want front or back?" His laugh sprays me with spit and whisky.

While the idea of double teaming a drunk hooker in the middle of the Texas desert with a guy who hasn't showered in months may be appealing to some, and a kink for others, I continue to decline graciously.

"You take her all on your own," I say. "You've been here longer. You've got seniority. Now, go get her, champ." I really just cheered on a guy to have sex with a strung out prostitute. New lows every day out here.

Then, looking around, it dawns on me that this may still be a test. If they suspect I'm not who I say I am they may be using this to test me. A clean law enforcement officer would never have sex with a prostitute. It's brilliant.

The Second is still outside his small house taking swigs from a bottle of Jack while the prostitution fumbles her hands all over him. I can't tell if he's watching me or if I'm over complicating the situation.

There's four guys now vying for three women that are left unclaimed in this perverted desert brothel. I grab two bottles of Jack from the dwindling supply and move in. Two of the women are fairly alert. Probably just drunk. They acknowledge my arrival to the party. The third women is staring into the air as if something is there that nobody else can see. Her teeth are yellow with black stains. She's my dream girl, for tonight at least.

I push through the group, and in between one of the men I'd beaten beside the bonfire and the crack-addled woman he was somehow unsuccessfully wooing.

"Sorry, bud. I got this one." I take her by the arm and walk away.

"What the fuck, man! I was gettin' somewhere with her!" he yelled after me.

"She's a hooker and has no idea where she is or what year it is, brother. If you couldn't close that deal then it wasn't gonna happen."

My plan is weak. Less than weak. Nonexistent is more like it. I keep walking with her while I think. She trips every three steps and I have to keep her vertical.

"Whatcha wanna do?" The words are slurred into one syllable.

"She speaks," I say. But that was the first and last thing she said.

I try the trailer, but there are already three guys and two

women in there. I grab the filthy mattress from my cot, mostly to keep them from using it during whatever it is they are about to do.

"Come on," I say, even though she has no idea what is happening. I can't keep from thinking about how I'll tell Eva about this. There's hardly any details I leave out when I finish a case while we sit on the balcony with drinks.

I take her past the last building and nobody is there. The open desert is just through the tall chain link fence and in some way could be considered romantic. I toss the mattress on the ground and lower her to it and sit beside her on the ground.

"So, here we are baby," I say.

She drools.

I was worried the walking around would straighten her out but it seems to have had the opposite reaction.

I open one of the bottles of Jack, take a swig, and hand it to her. With catlike reflexes, not a drop spilled, she takes it and puts it to her mouth. More of the dark liquid pours into her at once than I thought possible without taking a breath. It's like seeing a coma patient instantly wake up, speak perfectly to their loved one, then lay back into restless sleep again. Only she slams a quarter bottle of Jack then collapses against my left shoulder.

What I plan on doing tonight will be a low point in my life. Maybe the lowest. Even a prostitute looking for money for her next hit of crack doesn't deserve to be treated like I'm about to treat her.

CHAPTER 29

There's laughing and several loud "woohoo!'s" that wake me. I look up from the dirty cot on the ground to see most of the other guys grouped up and looking down at me. The Second is in the back of the pack. No "Woohoos" from him, but he does seem content.

The men in front begin with the comments.

"You did 'er good, didn't ya, new guy!"

"Damn, you didn't even share, you mother fucker."

Laying beside me is the prostitute. We are both naked, except for my socks and her bra which is pushed down under her ample bosom, nothing hidden.

I'd kept her drinking Jack until she passed out, which took into the second bottle. The next hour was spent making sure she was still alive and not dead from alcohol poisoning. Then I did what made me feel the worst. I took all of her clothes off, except for the aforementioned brassiere, which I pushed down under her breasts. I didn't want the scene to look too staged. I couldn't sleep after that, mostly out of guilt, but also out of concern she'd come to, get up, and go walking off away from my fake love den. Turns out there was no worry about that. Shortly before dawn and when I heard the first sounds of life in camp, I removed my clothes and took my place beside her, pulling one of her legs over mine in a pseudo post coital exhaustion position.

"Get out of here and let me have a turn before she wakes up." It's one of the men I haven't dealt with before.

I stand up in full nudity and nod down toward my nethers. "Don't think there's much left for you, brother." And I walk off to find a shower.

Nobody bothers me or even comes near for several hours, during which I sit in my shady spot to watch the goings-on of the camp and continue to size up my colleagues and competition. The women are carted off in the back of a black panel van. Even the few men I haven't directly had contact with are benign, at best. I've seen no weapons other than the stray pocket knife and the two assault rifles shared by whomever is on guard duty.

The van arrives with a cold dinner of hamburgers and hot dogs that taste like they were made three days ago. Nothing much happens for a few hours after that. The sun is down and the coolness that takes over the desert rolls in. It's never a sudden change in temperature. The breezes change until suddenly you realize you're cold.

The Second walks over to me. I'm in my usual spot

bothering nobody. A few other men linger behind him, not making eye contact with me.

"You're with us," the Second says.

I get up and follow them, no questions asked.

At the front gate a black Mercedes Sprinter van I've never seen before is idling. One of the other men takes the driver's seat, the rest of us climb in back and sit on the metal floor. There are two long black duffel bags over the wheel arches.

We are on the road for forty-five minutes at least when the van slows and turns off the pavement onto gravel. No words have been said. No orders or directions about what is going to happen. For all I know I failed the hooker test and am about to be killed and left in a west Texas field. I consider that idea and decide I don't like it.

Another half hour on gravel then what feels like just dirt, no road at all. The driver is down to under ten miles an hour and making adjustments in the dark to avoid holes and rocks. He's doing a bad job of it.

We stop.

The black duffels are opened and the other men each get an assault rifle or a pistol. I'm given a cheap 9mm similar to the one I'd shot with the Second. I didn't have to check the magazine. I could tell it was empty or only had a round or two in it by the weight of it in my hand. Still, I pop the magazine out, snap it back in, and pull the slide back to check the chamber. Two rounds. I watch as one of my trailer partners drops the magazine from his pistol and shows a slight grimace. My guess is it also isn't loaded or only has one or two rounds. Trust only goes so far.

The Second looks at me.

"Stay behind us. Don't talk. Don't do a goddamn thing. If someone flinches, you don't. If someone talks to you, you don't say a word. If shit goes down, shoot."

I nod to show how well I can listen.

In watching the tribe of a dozen men over the time I've been with them, I've established they are all criminals of one sort or another. Petty theft or assault and battery. Nothing so serious as to lock them up for more than a couple years at a time. Most have some form of ink that is obvious it was done in a dark cell with a handmade tool and a broken ballpoint pen, handled by a novice at best. One white guy even has a teardrop under his eye. If we were on the west coast, this would mean he murdered someone, or wanted people to think he had. But down here in Texas it might just be that he spent time inside, or worse, was raped in prison and marked by his attacker.

None of them are dangerous to me. I've beaten most of them in hand-to-hand and those that I haven't fought yet don't frighten me. The only worry is if they all ambush me at some point. I plan to not let that happen.

The side door of the van opens and I let all of the others out first and fall in behind them as ordered. A sliver of a moon offers the only light. Just as my eyes begin to see outlines of people and a vehicle, headlights blind me. There are two men that I can make out. Could be others farther back or outside the spray of the lights.

The Second steps forward. No hesitation. He's done this before, probably right here with the same silhouetted people facing him. He pulls a large envelope from his back pocket and tosses it into the bright lights where it's caught by the other man.

I hear the paper crinkle and the haloed head nods.

"It's all here," the man says.

I can see no features and make out no details about him. The voice is my first and only hint. I would say it is a white man in his thirties or forties. He has a drawl, but not Texan. Oklahoma maybe. Perhaps Arkansas. No farther north or east than that.

The man motions and two others come forward into the light. They are carrying a pair of boxes and hand them to two of our men.

Without anything else said, we all retreat to our own vehicles. As the van door is sliding shut, the other car turns to go out the other side of the field. It's a large pickup, a Dodge Ram by the shape of the hood, most likely. There's a light bar on the roof. Law enforcement of some kind.

It isn't until we are on the road that I can make out the shapes of the two boxes when headlights from an oncoming semi illuminates the inside of the van. They are matching, about eighteen inches square. There are markings I can't read, but they look military.

The ride back to camp is the same as the one out. No talking. Everyone gets out of the van and goes their own way to their trailers. I accept my new outdoor life and return to my cot at the back of the compound. I've slept in worse places, and it is far better than being inside the small trailer with three other smelly men and the unknown of what happened in there with the hookers.

As I listen to the creatures that only come out after dark, I think of the night's activity. You never know where a case will take you, and this one is no different.

CHAPTER 30

"Walk with me, Brother."

"Okay. And what do I call you?"

The man chuckles. "You can call me anything you wish, but most simply call me the Ruby."

The Second had woken me early. A bandana was poorly tied around my eyes as I was put into the front of the red pickup. The blindfold was unnecessary. I could tell we turned right out of the compound, drove about four miles, then turned left across a cattle guard and stopped no more than a quarter mile later.

There's an old white farmhouse on top of a rise in the land. Small barns and outbuildings dot the acreage behind it. A couple dozen men and women are moving about doing work. Some of it is obvious, such as mowing with an old style non-engined mower. Other activities are not so clear. A group of women walk from one building to another carrying white plastic containers like the postal service uses to sort mail.

"How long have you been there? At the camp," he says.

"Six days, I think. Maybe seven."

The Ruby had been standing in front of me when the Second pulled the blindfold off. The Ruby is shorter than me by half a foot, a bit round in the middle, white hair, and is again wearing a white shirt and white slacks.

"You have gone through the rites quickly," he says.

"Have I?"

"Oh, yes. You gave quite a performance at the cull. The men will be talking about that for a long time."

"The cull?" I say.

"The trial by combat. You were quite impressive."

"I'm glad I entertained."

"You did more than entertain." He motions to the Second to stay behind and we walk together past the buildings. "You impressed."

The people working weave around us, never forcing the Ruby to alter his path. Eyes are lowered in reverence and no words are spoken to him. They are dressed in simple matching clothes. The men have dark work pants and light blue longsleeved buttoned shirts. The women are in skirts the color of the men's pants and puffy blue blouses with long sleeves. They all look exceptionally clean, compared to the men at the compound down the road.

When we reach the fence separating the manicured grounds from the unkept pasture, the Ruby turns to look back up the hill. He takes in the people working and the buildings and has something different than a smile. Not quite a smirk. It is what you expect a king might do when looking out across his kingdom.

"Do you know who we are?"

I try to see what he sees and pretend I haven't read anything about them. "No. I don't."

He pauses and adjusts his stance. His body straightens, one foot moves slightly forward toward the landscape. It seems forced and perhaps intended only to add drama to the moment. His words come out rehearsed. "When man inherited this earth, he did not know what he had. The majesty, the miracle of the soil and the mountains, the seas and the canyons. He took it for granted and made it his own. He killed to take what he wanted from any who lived there before. Then that wasn't enough. They wanted control over each other and from that governments were born from the minds of the delusional, the power hungry self-important."

He is on a roll and I don't want to interrupt him but I feel I'm standing here listening to him narrate his manifesto to me. Can little cups of Kool-Aid be far behind?

"The first Ruby was chosen when the men saw the future of our land, our nation. He was a farmer, like myself, in the Blue Ridge mountains of Virginia. It was determined then that there would always be a Ruby, a keeper of the truth and proprietor of the future. Passed from Ruby to Ruby would be the ideals of how we must be as men, what we must become when the time is right, and what we as men must do if the oppression of the truth becomes what people think is the actual truth."

"The actual truth?" I say.

"Yes." He is pleased that I asked the question, as if I had read the script he kept in his mind. "The actual truth is the truth of the people. It is why we are here. Our purpose on this earth."

"Like, the meaning of life?" I say. "That purpose?"

He inhales as if about to speak, then pauses, turns to me, and shakes a finger at me as if he'd done it a hundred times.

"No, no, no," he says. "You almost fooled me. The Ruby is the keeper of the truth, and the Ruby alone must decide when the time is right to bring that truth to the world."

"So, you know what the meaning of life is?"

"I do."

"But you can't tell anyone."

"That is correct."

"Until the time is right to tell everyone."

"Not tell them, show them." He smiles a wide smile with the final words and begins to nod. I nod and smile with him and this once again pleases him. At this point Bigfoot riding a dinosaur walking out from behind the barn would make as much sense as anything he said.

He motions with his hand toward all the workers and buildings and the white farmhouse with the red roof.

"We are Ruby Rising."

There it is. The name from the LLC.

"And what does that mean exactly?"

"It means we have risen from the ashes of those who came before us, those who were punished for not falling in line, for being true believers and not giving in to the governments that forced their beliefs on their citizens.

Rubies before me have been persecuted, imprisoned, and murdered for possessing the truth."

I look off toward the workers and do my best impression of someone who knows what the hell he's talking about.

"Ruby Ridge. Branch Davidians," I say.

"Yes, to name a few." He grins and nods and for the first time looks like the true lunatic that he is.

"Was David Koresh the Ruby?"

He shakes his head. "No. He was a student of the Ruby before me, and perhaps could have been the next. But he lost his way."

"Is this a revenge group then? Like Tim McVeigh?"

"Far from it, and we condemn the work people like that do. We are here to do what the others were not able to. Their leaders became obsessed with power and confused themselves for saviors, prophets, gods."

"And you don't?"

"I do not."

"What are you, then, if not a prophet, yet you possess the meaning of life?"

"I'm a leader. I'm a brother. I'm a father. I'm a guide to the few who find me and earn their place beside me and do the work required of them to fulfill our mission, if it comes time."

"What work do you do?"

"We are liberators working to show the world there is another way, a way without government or oversight, police or armies. Just peace."

"Peace? But you sponsor trailer park brawls to choose your followers?"

"Our work is at times difficult. Physical sometimes. We need men strong of mind and body. Look how everyone here exists in harmony."

I look at the men and women in their matching outfits, silently carrying and cleaning and mowing.

"Who are these people?"

"These are The Arm of the Ruby. The followers. The students."

"Very utopian. What does that make us at the compound?"

"You, my brother, are the fighters, the martyrs. You are the Sword at the End of the Arm."

CHAPTER 31

A table is set up with two chairs on the porch of the white farmhouse. The Ruby motions for me to sit and I do. The red pickup is still in the driveway but the Second is not in sight. As soon as we are seated, two women come out with glass carafes of orange juice and coffee. Fresh baked scones and croissants are presented and I take one of each, then several pieces of bacon and some eggs from a platter placed between us. The meals at the compound are barely edible and I capitalize on the offerings in front of me.

"Yes, yes," the Ruby says. "Eat. Fill yourself."

I nod with a piece of bacon half out of my mouth.

"You have proven yourself beyond any others from the Sword ever have," he says.

"What about the Second?" I say. "He leads your little army. He must have proven himself as well."

"He has, but in a different way. He maintains the status quo and finds new men when they are needed. He keeps you and the others hungry and eager."

"Some of the men think that if they perform well enough they will be able to move to the ranch," I say. "Is that true? Has anyone ever moved from the compound to the ranch?"

The Ruby looks out across the field beside the farmhouse. "It is not true, if I am to be honest. It is not an offer or promise that is ever expressly stated, but if some of the men hear it and think it to be true, it only increases their desire to serve."

A young woman brings more coffee and sets it on the table. The Ruby puts his hand on her arm and smiles up at her. She looks down into his eyes and I see a little of what I see when Eva looks at me.

"The people here, do they love you?"

"You would have to ask them that." He laughs. "I never ask for their love or make it a requirement of their position in the group. If they do, then all the better, because I love each and every one of them."

A woman walks by, her hands beneath her extended pregnant belly. I look at her then at the Ruby. "You love all of them?"

"I am still a man, my brother. Flesh and blood with desires and needs," he says. "I never ask of anyone what they do not want for themselves. I had another life before this, before I was called on to be the Ruby. I was married and had two children, but that ended. It was a different world, a different incarnation of me. Now I'm just an old man trying to make a better world for the people who choose to be near me."

"What do you do for them?" I say. "What do you do that makes them love you, or at the minimum, follow you and stay here?"

He sips his coffee slowly then sits back and ponders the question, or acts as if he is. With a loud exhale, he answers.

"I offer a place to belong, to be free. To love and be loved. To work hard and reap the benefits of that work. I keep them safe from the evils of the world around us as best I can."

"Do you offer them salvation?"

"No, that I do not. I am not a religious man by nature. My mother was and instilled in me the fire-and-brimstone God of her own youth and the people she followed. I never liked that and eschewed it as soon as I could and never darkened the doorway of a place of worship again. We have an area here we call the chapel for those who wish to practice their own religions, but I do not oversee or preach to them."

"What are your requirements to be admitted, then? To be part of Ruby Rising."

"Only to want to be here of your own will, and to take part in all of the daily work it takes to keep everybody fed and content, and I hope happy."

"Does anyone ever leave?"

"Rarely."

He answers everything I ask easily. With as many interrogations I have been a part of, I can sense a liar, and I do not feel he is being dishonest. In his own way he loves these people. I watch as everyone works, and though it is weird to me, it all looks natural to them. I see them stop and chat with each other, help each other, and work hard. Nobody has the glazed over looks and spooky smiles you expect to see from cult members, the vision of them engrained in us by movies and television shows.

"What about us, then? The Sword at the End of the Arm," I say. "How are we different than the followers here? We are kept separate. We're kept dirty and hungry. We are made to fight each other. Do you love us?"

"I am the first incarnation of the Ruby to have such a defined Sword. In the past it has been two or three members of the main group who assist the Ruby with some of the tasks that are not as, well, clean."

"The illegal stuff," I say. "The stuff that brings in the money to support all of this."

He nods slowly, cautiously.

"That is oversimplified, but yes. As times change, as the world changes around us, we must adapt. I saw a need for a more structured approach to fundraising and protection. The Second had recently come to us and was not fitting into the larger group, as you might expect by knowing him. I pulled him aside and tasked him with creating the Sword we have today."

"How does the Nepali fit in?"

"You don't miss much," he says. "He is the latest in a long line of assistants to the Rubies. It is their family honor to serve. His methods are crude, I admit, but he keeps his dealings away from here and does what he needs to keep us safe. The Second worked with him to find the first group of men for the new iteration of the Sword in Arizona some time back."

The connection to Yuma. They were brought in as hired guns, essentially.

"We are beginning a new era to our time here," he says. "Embarking into new territory. It has been a long path to reach the decision to move forward, but the evils of the outside world and the pressures upon us have forced me. There is a cloud over us, and we must protect ourselves."

"What new era? What are you going to do?"

"You will find out soon enough. Your arrival and skills helped me to feel better about the choices I've had to make these last few days, and you will be an important part of our mission."

CHAPTER 32

After breakfast and the near luxury of the ranch, I am returned to the compound, once again blindfolded. The Second is more silent than even he usually is. Upon arrival I'm released from the truck. Before I can even get to a tree to relieve myself of the four cups of coffee, the Second pulls five of us aside from the rest of the group. The other four quickly seem excited, like they know what is happening.

"Is it time, boss?"

The Second nods. The men yell and celebrate.

"Okay, okay. We must remain calm in our service to the Ruby. This is an honor, a privilege, that you have been chosen."

The man I know only as Gerry points to me. "What's he doing here? He hasn't been here long enough to trust him."

"He was hand picked by the Ruby and we'll all accept

him as part of the mission," the Second says. "Tomorrow we'll go to the ranch to prepare."

"The ranch?" The men mutter. "Never been to the ranch."

"Really? It's nice," I say, which doesn't help me earn any friends.

I can only think that the hookers were in fact a final test and that I passed. It would be a story for Gus over beers at the bar. I have to consider if it is one for Eva on the balcony.

I spend the afternoon thinking about the Ruby and his followers. They live in complete contrast to the guys here at the compound. It is hard to imagine the ones I saw taking up arms or being violent at all. They really did seem like they had found what they were looking for. The question is has the Ruby found what he wanted?

It's difficult for me to outright call that a cult, based on how most people imagine them. By textbook definition, sure. I'm more inclined to say a commune. But in the end, if this all goes badly, all the news will ever call them is a cult.

The group here under command of the Second is far from a cult and not quite a militia, either. These are lifelong criminals looking for somewhere to live, to feel safe, to earn their keep. They don't care which side of the law that sits on. They are content letting someone else plan everything, provide the food, the drink, and yes, even the hookers.

After dinner Gerry corners me, complete with poking me in my chest. While listening to him talk I occupy my time thinking of each way I could break his finger.

"You better watch yourself, buddy," he says. "I been here

for eight months and am finally getting my shot. If you get in my way or screw anything up, I'll finish you."

In my periphery I see the Second come out of his room, his eyes quickly locking on us.

I don't want Gerry messing up the mission for me, so I decide to remove him from it. I look him up and down.

"Hey, I heard from one of the hookers that you couldn't get it up," I say.

His response is so immediate and violent that I have to wonder if it is actually true. He swings with a telegraphed left cross that has no power to it, his shoulder going so far back to start the punch that I have time to take a nap before the fist gets anywhere near me. It would be fun to take him down. I haven't faced off with him yet. But that isn't my endgame with him. I have to take one for the mission. I move with the swing and let it glance off my chin. I go to the ground with more force than the strike to my face.

The Second is on us and pulling Gerry away from me. He glances at me and just shakes his head. A few others drag Gerry back while he tries to free himself to get more of me.

The Second removes his hat and runs his hand through thinning blond hair. I may have made it too obvious.

"Walk with me," he says.

We do a lap of the perimeter inside the fence.

"This isn't an easy job, you know," he says.

"Never thought it was. Whatever it is. I have no idea actually. Could be easy. Could be hard."

"Just shut up and listen sometimes, will ya? The Ruby

puts a lot of pressure on me to find good men, capable men, who will listen and do what is expected of them."

"I can imagine."

"Now, I know not all of them buy into everything the Ruby says. Hell, I'm not sure I do. But we have a good thing going here. Most of these guys couldn't pay rent or get a job good enough to even feed themselves. This may not be Shangri-fucking-la here, but it's a roof over their heads and three squares a day."

"Not to mention the hookers."

He laughs. "And the hookers."

We get to the back corner of the compound. On the other side of the fence is the longest stretch of open land in the area. You can walk fifteen, maybe twenty miles without hitting a road or a house or even a fence. Most of it is privately owned but some is just wild land not worth owning.

"Why'd you let him slug you?"

"What's that?" I say.

"Back there. Why'd you let Gerry slug you?" It's the first time I've heard him use one of the men's names.

"I have no idea what this mission is," I say, "but what I do know is I don't want to get shot in the back of the head or put in a no-win situation by a butthurt redneck who knows he's not as good as the rest of the team."

"So you knew I was watching and figured you'd take the slug and he'd get thrown off the mission."

"Something like that. Well, exactly that."

He nods. "You know, I don't even know whether to trust you yet. You piss off everyone here, beat all our asses in the fights, take a hooker for yourself when the rest of 'em have to share, and somehow have the Ruby thinking your shit don't stink."

"It does. Trust me. With the food they bring us?"

"This mission is serious, and I need to know if you are part of the team or just here as some kind of joke."

"I'm here, aren't I."

CHAPTER 33

I go to my dark corner of the compound and watch as the men each disappear to their trailers or fall asleep beside the fire. The Second went into his room shortly after our walk. Two sentries are still posted at the front gate and I know they don't rotate new men in for another four hours.

Gus is the camper. He can go out into the wild for a week with only what he carries in and actually enjoy himself. I'm okay taking a nice hike then retiring to a hotel room with a comfortable bed. But being out here has me rethinking the whole outdoors thing. I won't tell Gus, but I'm enjoying seeing the wide sky above me at night. Austin doesn't have the light pollution of bigger cities, but it is still enough that you only see the most prominent constellations and bright planets when visible. But here, it's everything. To look up and see into the depths of the universe is humbling and mind numbing. Though I do find myself wondering if there's anything out there looking back.

One time I went SCUBA diving with some agents when we were in the Bahamas for a weekend. Gus wasn't with us, being assigned to the field office in Chicago, but as much as he loves outdoor life, you can't get him thirty feet below water with a tank on his back. He says it's unnatural. Most of us weren't certified to dive, but we'd lied to the dive company and I'm sure one of the guys flashed a badge, paid the dive operator off, or both, but we were allowed to gear up and jump off the boat.

We'd leveled off at about forty-five feet and three of us were following the one guy who was certified, as well as being a divemaster and instructor. He'd told us all we needed to know on the van ride to the other side of the island to meet the boat. I'm sure it wasn't the safest thing, but we were all adults.

I was in the back of the group, taking my time and looking down at the plant life and the fish swimming past. A grouper the size of a small car looked at us then continued on its way, and I'm pretty sure I saw a barracuda that decided we weren't worth her time.

I look ahead and see the other four guys stopped, vertical in the water as if they could stand on some imaginary floor. I watched them as I continued on, wondering what they were doing, then one of them motioned down. I stopped kicking and looked down again. Beneath me was the deepest shade of black I've ever seen. At some point since noticing they'd stopped, I'd swam past the edge of a shelf, over into what is known as the Great Bahama Canyon. It was the smallest

I've ever felt. Unknown things live down in that darkness, unknown to me at least and perhaps even to scientists who study such things.

That's the exact opposite of looking up at the stars out here with no city lights causing them to be invisible. Where the ocean gave me the fear of hyperventilating and drowning, the open sky relaxes me.

The harsh scent of bad weed pulls me back from the stars. Someone has a stash and is partaking. My guess is the sentries, which only helps me. I don't know how they think they are being secretive about it when the stink spreads throughout the whole compound.

In my nights sleeping outside behind the last building, I've found a gap at the bottom of the fence. It isn't a comfortable fit, but with a few scratches from wire, I slip under and make sure it looks closed again.

With four hours until guard change, I move quickly once I'm out of sight of the camp. I have no flashlight and the ground is rough. I trip a couple times but luckily don't have any scratches to explain to anyone at the camp.

After two miles in the darkness, I reach my landmark. It's an old electric pole a good thirty feet off the dirt road left over from a building that has long ago become part of the desert again. Before letting myself get taken to the compound, I'd hidden my security blanket here.

I sit down on the ground beside where my stash is hidden and sit quietly for several minutes, listening to the plains for signs of footsteps that followed me or a car coming down the road. Once I feel safe, I brush the dirt off the top of the military issue ammo box.

Inside is a Glock 19 with three loaded magazines, and a satellite phone wrapped in a plastic bag. The gun is from an evidence box at the San Antonio field office and can't be traced back to me, aside from my fingerprints on it.

I open the phone, listen to the air again, then dial.

"Eddie?"

"Who else would it be?"

"Good to hear your voice. Are you safe?"

"I am. I snuck away to call and only have a couple minutes."

"Then catch me up quick," Gus says.

I give him the rundown on the camp, the Second, the Ruby, and the ranch. I don't go into detail about the meaning of life but sum it up by saying I'm pretty sure the Ruby is up to no good.

"I've been chosen for a mission," I say. "We go to the ranch in the morning for preparations. That's all I know. Don't know when we leave for the mission, where it is, what it is."

"Is it too dangerous to keep the satellite phone with you?"

"Yeah. Wouldn't risk it. Do you have any way to keep eyes on me?"

"I'm about ten miles away right now," Gus says. "We have a few drones we were waiting to use. Will have to keep them at high altitude so they won't be heard, but will be good enough to know where you are."

"The guards at the compound will never notice. I didn't see as much of a guard presence at the ranch, but I'm sure there's something," I say. "Hold on a second."

I lower the phone and cup my hand over the earpiece to listen to the plains for footfalls or voices, then raise it to my ear again.

"And I hope you're sitting down," I say. "The Nepali is here."

"What?" Gus says. "Where? How?"

"He was with the Ruby when they came to the compound for the fights, but I didn't see him at the ranch this morning. But I'm sure he's still around."

"You think he recognized you?"

"Can't say. He saw me fight."

"If he's recognized you, then you've been made. Watch your back."

"I will, trust me," I say. "I'll try to call if I can, but won't be from the sat phone. Otherwise, I hope you can track me."

"We'll do our best."

"Call Eva for me? Tell her I love her sweet boobies and hope to nuzzle them soon."

"I won't do that but I'll tell her you're safe."

"Good enough."

I hang up and listen to the night again. Still silent. I wrap the phone and place it back in the ammo box and take the Glock in my hand just to feel the weight and the sense of security it offers. I've spent years of my left with a similar weapon on my side at all times. I've used that weapon too often and taken lives with it. It is never a decision I take lightly, but always when it is their life or mine at stake. Working with the Joint Terrorism Task Force and being a part of missions to bomb areas of desert in Afghanistan was always harder to me than pulling a trigger to kill a man. When you order a bomb strike or a team of SEALs to go in, it isn't an act of immediate self defense. Yes, it is to protect our country, or so we tell ourselves. But in the end it is hard to differentiate from sanctioned murder.

Back through the darkness, I stop short of the camp and watch for movement, then slip back under the fence and roll right onto my mattress just as footsteps come from around the building.

"Where the fuck were you, asshole? Was just here looking for you."

I look up at the man. "I had to take a piss and prefer not to do it right beside where I sleep. What the hell are you bothering me for?"

"The Second is looking for you. It's time to load up."

CHAPTER 34

I follow the man to the front of the camp. The black Mercedes Sprinter van is parked sideways outside the gate. The Second and the three other men on the mission are waiting.

"Glad you decided to join us," the Second says.

Two of the men are putting on coveralls with an electric company logo on the back. The third is in a San Antonio police uniform. The Second has on a dark grey suit, white shirt, and black tie. His hair is brushed back.

"Put these on." The Second hands me a bag.

Inside are a pair of cargo shorts and a bright yellow L.A. Lakers LeBron James jersey. I look at it for a moment and hear the other men laughing. Luckily I have a white T-shirt on and pull the jersey over it so I don't have to walk around sleeveless.

"Looks good on you," the Second says.

"Thanks. I think."

The men start to climb in the side of the Sprinter van and I follow.

"Not so fast," the Second says. "You're with me."

We walk to the other side of the van and the beater Corolla I'd driven to the camp is sitting there. The first thing I notice is the license plates have been changed out with ones from California. I see a theme building here.

"You drive," the Second says.

The keys are in the ignition and the car starts rough.

"Will it make it?" he says.

"Depends on how far we're going."

"I'll tell you what you need to know. Just follow the van for now."

"We aren't going to the ranch?"

"Nope."

I do what he says. Eventually we are on I-10 headed east toward Austin. The state capitol building. Plenty of other important offices. The university. I keep working through potential targets in my mind as I drive. But as far as I know the target could be an ATM at a convenience store.

I watch my rearview mirror as casually as possible for signs of Gus. I just hope he was in place in time to see us leave.

We get to the split to 290 toward Austin but stay on I-10 to San Antonio. A new list of targets forms in my head. The Alamodome. The Tower of the Americas. The Riverwalk and the Alamo filled with tourists.

The Second is beside me giving instructions and having me

repeat them back, down to what parking space to use, which doors to go in and out of, what to say, and where to meet up later. None of it is difficult and nothing sounds dangerous.

Nothing the Ruby said to me made me think they would do anything huge. He condemned the actions of the Oklahoma City bombers. But still, we are loaded up and headed into a metropolitan area.

As we enter the city and work our way downtown, the Second pulls a small paper bag from the back seat.

"You'll have a few hours to wait. Get to your parking spot and sit in the car until it is time to go. 11:45. Got it?"

"Got it."

"This is for your wait and for the meetup," he says. "Pull over at the next corner."

The van continues on and I pull to the curb. The Second opens the passenger door.

"I'll see you in a few hours," he says.

Then the door is closed and he walks down the street in his gray suit and cowboy boots.

My first thought is to get to a phone and call Gus. But I don't know if they have someone following me or a tracking device in the car. I just hope there is a chance at my destination to contact him.

A few minutes later I'm parked in the exact space the Second told me to use, in an outside lot, backed in, the exit to the street only a few car lengths away. It's a perfect getaway spot, though I don't feel my assignment is anything I'll have to get away from.

I open the paper bag, not knowing what to expect. Inside is an egg sandwich, a bag of potato chips, and a $20 bill.

I check the time. 9:15. A long time to go. I pace myself with the sandwich and tuck the money in one of the many pockets in my cargo shorts and hope I can remember later which one.

The air conditioner of course doesn't work in the car, so I sit with the windows down. A few people walk past and look at me, but nobody bothers me. I try to nap but it's too hot and I want to stay alert. I watch the road in front of me for the Sprinter van but it never passes.

I consider stopping someone walking past to see if I can use their cellphone, but decide against it.

Finally, at 11:45, I leave the car behind. The building the Second told me to enter is directly behind me about a hundred yards and to the left of the round U.S. District Courts building. I time my steps to when someone is exiting the side door of the building. I catch the door and go in, bypassing security screening at the front. It was too easy to enter a district court building without being stopped.

I climb the three flights of stairs and enter the hallway. The office I'm looking for is only a few feet away. I push the door open and go in.

There are four desks with nobody sitting at them and a small office in the back. I can hear movement.

Two minutes. That's how long I need to be in here. No more. No less. The Second was very clear about that.

"Hello?"

The sound of a chair scooting on the tiled floor, and a head appears around the doorframe of the office.

"We're closed for lunch. Come back after 1:00."

I need to delay for at least ninety more seconds.

"I just have a couple questions," I say.

"And my assistants will be happy to answer them after 1:00." He's no longer visible in the door.

"Who are you?" I'm grasping to kill time.

The chair scrapes loudly again and the man comes out of the office with a sandwich in one hand.

"I'm Assistant District Attorney Culver and you are interrupting my lunch." He looks at my shirt. "Lakers? Seriously? Just get out of here, will ya?"

"It was a gift. What does an Assistant District Attorney do?" I say.

"Please leave."

I look at him and weigh my options with sixty more seconds to kill and no idea what the other four men on the mission are up to, or if Gus knows where I am. He is, after all, an Assistant District Attorney, so I decide to trust him.

"Listen. I'm Special Agent Eddie Holland. I'm undercover and out of contact with my handler. Please get hold of SAC Gus Ramirez through the San Antonio field office. It's urgent. Just tell him I was here and the mission is at the district courts, and don't tell anyone other than him."

His sandwich is suspended halfway to his mouth as he had prepared to take another bite when I unloaded on him. Then he starts laughing.

"That's the best one I've heard. Now get the fuck out of my office before I call security. I'm due in court in less than an hour and I'd really like to enjoy my shitty sandwich before that."

"I'm serious."

"So am I."

I turn to leave, not wanting to risk security getting called. Back into the stairwell and I run down the three flights. As I get to the bottom, a San Antonio uniformed officer is starting up the stairs. I almost run into him.

"Where's the fire?" he says.

"Sorry, officer. Just late for court."

"For what? Wearing that jersey?" He laughs and starts up the stairs.

I'm out the side door of the building and a few minutes later back in the Corolla. I turn the key and the engine groans. I try again, same thing. I know it isn't a great car, but it ran fine on the drive from Austin over a week ago.

The clock on the dash says 11:58. I'm supposed to meet the Second at 12:45. I try the ignition one more time and it sputters then turns over. I know San Antonio well enough to get through downtown to the meeting place.

When I'm two blocks away, a police car screams past me headed toward the direction I came from. Then a second one. Before long, downtown is filled with sirens echoing off buildings. I continue on Cesar Chavez to I-10 North, then take Commerce west for several miles. The Second told me to stay off the highway, but I knew it would save a few minutes and with all the police activity, I wanted away from the downtown area.

I find the address he gave me. It's a small sports bar. Seems an odd place to meet up after a mission, but I'm a good little follower. I sit at the bar and order a beer. The $20 bill in the paper bag makes sense now. I look around the place. There's a few people sitting at tables eating and watching whatever is on the multiple televisions.

I'm tempted to order some food, figuring whatever they serve here is better than what we have in camp, but decide not to. After a few sips of my beer I hear a few people behind me talking loud and ask the waitress to turn the volume up on the TV.

I look up. All I see is an aerial view of the building I'd just been in and the round U.S. District Court building beside it. A reporter comes on.

"*There are reports of shots being fired inside the court building,*" the reporter says. "*It was hysteria as the buildings lost power and were evacuated, causing some injuries.*"

I get the waitress's attention. "Hey, could I borrow the phone?" It's time to risk it and call Gus.

"Not with that shirt on," she says. I notice her Spurs T-shirt. Of course.

I check the time on one of the news stations. 12:51. The Second is late. Was he caught? What was he caught doing?

The reporter comes back on.

"*A source from San Antonio police department on the scene has informed us that an Assistant District Attorney has died,*" he says. "*Bernard Culver was found dead in his office from an apparent gunshot wound.*"

Culver. I think back to the office I went to. The sign on the door. Bernard Culver. Something doesn't feel right.

"*A San Antonio police officer is reported to have been found dead of knife wounds in a stairwell near Mr. Culver's office.*"

They are getting some very specific information and very quickly.

"Can I get the check?" I say. Time to leave, with or without the Second.

"Police have provided a description and a photograph of a suspect in the death of Mr. Culver and the officer. Male, about five foot ten, and wearing a Los Angeles Lakers jersey, bright yellow, with the number 23 on it."

The screen switches away from live video of the people outside the courts, to a security camera video of me getting into the Corolla. I'm dead center in the middle of the frame.

Voices behind me. A chair moves. I look over my shoulder to see two men looking at me.

"This suspect was seen on the same floor as Mr. Culver's office, in the stairwell, and of course in this security camera footage fleeing the scene."

Fleeing the scene. Nice.

I drop the $20 on the counter and leave before I have to fight my way out.

CHAPTER 35

I'm in the Corolla and headed north, staying off main roads for now. The yellow jersey is in the parking lot where the car was parked beside the sports bar. The radio doesn't work so I can't listen for updates. Right now the only person who has seen the news and knows I am innocent is Gus. Hopefully some others who know about my undercover operation do, too.

With a dead San Antonio cop, I can't go to a police station or be caught by an officer. That wouldn't end well for me. I can stop at a pay phone and try to call Gus, but I just left all the money I had back at the bar.

I think of the city and move it around in my head until I know where to go. The Corolla blends in, but it's all over the news what I'm driving and likely the California plates.

I head east, back toward the courts, but more importantly

toward I-10. Driving easy, not speeding, I make it to the access road and go north. Fourteen miles. That's all I need. Fourteen long miles.

It's about two miles in when I see the first cruiser. It comes up onto the highway from a ramp. In my mirror the officer seems to not notice me. I'm in the right lane trying to stay surrounded by cars and the cruiser makes its way to the left lane and accelerates.

As it is passing me two lanes away, I glance over just as the officer looks to his right. There's about two beats before his eyes go wide.

There's an exit on the right for Culebra Road and I swerve onto it, barely missing the wall. I hear screeching tires and car horns behind me for I can only assume the officer slammed on his brakes to get over to the exit. I pass two cars on the off ramp and fly down to the bottom, look both ways at Culebra Road without stopping, and floor it across the intersection and back onto the long on ramp for I-10 again.

As I merge back onto the highway, I see the cruiser just getting onto the off ramp. If he sees me and follows, I gained some distance on him, which he can get back quickly with the powerful motor of the Dodge Charger. If he didn't see me, he's radioing every cruiser in five square miles right now, which he'll be doing either way.

There's no time for blending in. I put the pedal to the floor and the old Corolla doesn't really do much. But it's trying. I build up speed slowly and pass the few cars I'm going faster than. Eventually I'm up to 90 miles per hour in the left lane and feeling good. Not about the car, but that

I might actually make it. The car feels like it's going to fall apart under me.

It's another few miles before the next cruiser sighting. To make things worse, it's three cruisers all entering at the same time. If they haven't made me yet, they will any moment now. The Corolla is giving me all it can, and I ask for more. The temperature and oil lights are both on and I'm almost out of gas.

There's enough traffic that even the powerful cruisers take a few minutes to catch up to me. They will try to surround me first and make me slow down. If I don't, one of them will try the PIT maneuver, the *Pursuit Intervention Technique*. Essentially one of them will come from the side and tap the back of my car with the front of theirs, sending me into a flat spin. That's the good outcome. The bad outcome is the Corolla flips end over end down the highway, ejecting me along the way and probably killing me. The PIT maneuver at anything over 35 miles per hour is considered lethal.

The cruisers have caught up with their lights on and sirens blaring. Two are behind me and the third is coming up beside me on the right. I need about three more miles. At this speed, that's a little more than two minutes.

The last thing I want to do is injure a police officer. They're doing their job. They have no idea I'm innocent and that I actually know who is responsible. But unless I get to my destination, that information may never get out.

Two miles.

It's time to start moving over but I'm surrounded by cruisers on either side. There is no cruiser in front of me yet, but get real, I'm maxed out and going no faster. I swerve right and the cruiser swerves with me, almost hitting a car we are speeding past in the next lane over. I know that police protocol for high speed chases says he has to back off to keep from causing a crash, and he does. The next lane is clear now and I take it.

My exit will be difficult. As soon as I get down to safer speeds, the cruisers will ram me or attempt the PIT.

One mile.

I get to the far right lane. Two cruisers are now in line behind me, assuming I'm preparing to exit and not wanting to get caught in the wrong lane like the first cruiser. The third is staying two lanes over to my left to possibly force me to exit.

I need some distance and some cover. I reach down beside the seat to feel for a trunk release but don't find one. Next I check the remote on the keychain. Bingo. I hit the button for the trunk, and nothing. I try again. Still nothing. I hold it down and shake it. The trunk finally flies open.

One of the cruisers hits his brakes, likely thinking something is about to come flying out of the trunk.

Next, I turn on cruise control and set it to my current speed, which is about 82 miles per hour as I begin to slow.

I know this exit, and think about my options. The only one I can come up with involves me hitting the ground really hard from a fast speed. I'm not a fan of it, but it will have to work.

I slam on my brakes as hard as I can. The front tires lock up. All three cruisers follow suit and brake, but with full control of their vehicles. I put my foot back on the gas and angle right onto the exit to Frontage Road. I just need a few seconds out of the cruiser's visibility.

All I have as an option is a pair of hard left turns. A right would be better, thanks to gravity and g-forces and all, but the lefts will have to work.

After full throttle down the ramp, I brake and make the first hard left into the turnaround lane, a special lane for cars to U-Turn and head back the opposite direction on the other side of the highway. The cruisers give me some distance with other cars around now. They can catch up in seconds when they are ready to run me off the road.

The second left comes up quickly. I push open my door and as I turn left do several things at the same time.

As soon as I straighten the car out of the turn, my body begins to exit the vehicle with the door trying to close against me. I keep my foot on the gas to stay over 25 miles per hour, the minimum speed for most cars to use cruise control, and then tap the "resume" button on the steering wheel just as I release my grip and let myself fall to the ground, rolling on the pavement and onto the grass at near 30 miles per hour. I lunge out of the road toward the wall below the highway and flatten out in the grass, hoping the cruiser will be looking forward to the now accelerating Corolla, and not at the broken man on the ground beside the road.

I watch the car speed off without me inside. It stays straight on Frontage Road. I feel a pang of guilt for letting a car go off on its own with the inherent ability to hurt or kill innocent people.

A cruiser makes the corner and catches up to the car, unaware of the lack of occupant and with a clear two-lane road ahead of him. Like clockwork he comes in from the side, taps the rear of the Corolla, and sends it spinning off down the road where it settles on the front lawn of a new Toyota dealership. That's what I call synergy. My guilt for sending the speeding Corolla off on its own fades.

I have distance to cover and my body feels like it just flew out of a moving car, but I get going. I remove my T-shirt and carry it to change my appearance. Fortunately, a man walking on the side of the road with no shirt on is not uncommon in Texas, so it is not a shabby disguise.

Passing the Toyota dealership, several cruisers are pulled up, officers have guns drawn and aimed at the Corolla. Thank you, little car. You did good.

I cut through the back lot of the dealership, thinking that's the last place they would look for me. And I was right. For a few minutes. I get around the corner and am approaching the guard booth outside an office building as two officers on foot start yelling to me and a cruiser comes past them toward me.

Running up to the guard booth, a fit young man in a tight uniform opens the door. He looks at me then at the police officers that are quickly catching up to me.

"You're the guy from the news," he says.

"I'm Special Agent Eddie Holland and I need to see SAC Gus Ramirez before these officers catch me."

CHAPTER 36

The handcuffs are loose on my wrist. A courtesy from the local agents. The chain is long enough I can still raise the coffee to my mouth. It tastes horrible but I'm on my third cup.

Gus comes into the interrogation room along with Special Agent In Charge Hudson of the San Antonio field office and Chief of Police William Ranson.

"Can someone tell me why we're in here with my murder suspect?" Chief Ranson says.

"Because he's not your murder suspect," Gus says. "We need the security of the interrogation room to try to keep the information you are about to hear from getting out."

"What information? I have surveillance video, an eye witness, and the murder weapon that all say he killed my officer and the ADA."

"What murder weapon?" I say.

"A gun. A Hi-Point C-9 9mm with three rounds missing," the Chief says. "One in the attorney, the other two fired in the courts building."

"It's a plant," I say. "The Second took me shooting last week. He wore gloves and asked if I could handle a gun. I fired off a few rounds. After, he put it back in a holster, still wearing gloves."

"And who are you again, aside from maybe possibly being my murder suspect, but maybe not?" The Chief says.

"Eddie, please catch the Chief up." Gus gives me the floor.

"Chief. My name is Eddie Holland. I work for the FBI out of Austin and have been undercover with a cult-like group near Salt Creek. Special Agent Ramirez here is my handler and SAC Hudson is party to the mission."

Chief Ranson looks around the room at the different men, in disbelief. "Why the hell wasn't I informed of activity in my city, then?"

"We didn't know," Gus said. "Due to the nature of the mission, Eddie has been out of contact for well more than a week. I received a call from him last night simply saying something was happening, but he had no information other than that. We saw movement from the camp using a drone and moved to follow the vehicles in question."

"There's more than one vehicle?" Chief Ranson says.

"Yes, sir. Eddie here was driving the now infamous Corolla, while the other men were in a black Mercedes Sprinter van."

"Where are these other men?"

"We don't know," Gus says.

"Quite an operation you have going on. The one guy you think is innocent is in handcuffs and the guys you think did it are in the wind."

"We're working on that," Gus says. "For now we have to ask for your cooperation to keep from destroying all the work Special Agent Holland has done to this point. If he gets hauled in to jail, we lose control of him and the operation. The targeted group may have people inside the police force that would move to terminate him."

"You think I have bad cops?"

"Show me a force that doesn't have at least one and I'll give you a fucking lollipop." Gus is ready to move on and the Chief is in his way. "We don't need your permission, but time is of the essence so your assistance is appreciated. Now do we have your cooperation or not?"

The Chief looks at me. "Why is he in cuffs if he's innocent?"

"To look guilty. We're not taking any chances that we don't have an informant in our own office. We need him to be seen in custody."

"What's next then?" Chief Ranson says.

"You make a statement to the press that the suspect has been apprehended and that you have asked the FBI to hold him in order to keep him protected, due to the nature of his crime. From there, we handle Special Agent Holland and get the people who really killed those two men."

There's a knock on the door. SAC Hudson opens it. A young agent is there.

"Sir, we need you," he says.

"What is it?" SAC Hudson says.

"Information out of the courts building, sir. Seems there's a problem there."

"I don't have time for twenty questions. What kind of problems?"

The young agent looks at the Chief then back to Hudson.

"The locals lost a defendant who was brought over from the jail for a court hearing."

"Sounds like this is the Chief's problem, not ours," Hudson says.

"It may be both."

A laptop is brought into the interrogation room and we gather around it to watch security footage from the district court building. People are coming in through the security checkpoint. Others stand and talk in the lobby.

"There," I say. "Those two in the coveralls. They're from the compound. They had uniforms from an electrician's shop."

The two men are each carrying a black bag with tools sticking out of the sides. They are too small on the screen to make out much more. Three minutes after that I point out the Second going through security. He showed identification and was breezed through. I tap the space bar to pause the video.

"Who gets through the checkpoint that easily?" I say.

"It's not our jurisdiction," the Chief says. "But from being in that building more than I'd like I can tell you that police officers and attorneys are barely looked at twice as long as they have the right ID."

I look at the Second on the video in his gray suit and wispy blond hair brushed back.

"He had Bernard Culver's ID," I say. "That explains the timing."

"What do you mean?" Gus says.

"He wanted me in and out of the neighboring building before noon but we weren't meeting back up until 12:45."

"So?"

"He needed time for someone to go back into the office, kill Culver and take his ID, and get it over to him at the main building so he can walk right in. I was just a pawn. There would be video of me going in and that's all that would get released, framing me for the murder, which was carried out by someone else."

"The Nepali," Gus says.

"Who the hell is the Nepali?" The Chief says.

"Long story," I say. "But a bad guy. A really bad guy. He likely killed the ADA and the officer then hightailed it over to give the Second the ID. The cop was unplanned, that's why he resorted to his blade. He'd already planted the gun in the ADA's office. I know all the men on the mission and don't think any of them are capable of carrying this out. Had to be the Nepali."

"Why did the Second need to get in the district courts building, and do we not have a name on him yet?" Gus says. "I'm feeling silly calling him the Second."

"We don't have a name yet, but I'm guessing the Ruby had him help a convict escape. If we look up the escapee's court time, I'll bet you the prosecutor is the one and only Bernard Culver."

I unpause the video. Six minutes after the Second enters the building, the lobby goes dark. You can still make out shapes moving, but not enough to identify anyone.

"What happened there?" Hudson says.

"Power outage, sir," the young agent says. "The courts building lost all electricity for about ten minutes."

"How is there still video?" I say.

"Court security found a pair of devices in the electric control room. They're not sure what they are, but the seem to have disrupted only the main power source for the building. The security system is outsourced and on its own grid."

"An EMP," I say. "That's what they bought in the field a few nights ago."

"An electromagnetic pulse?" Gus says.

"Just enough to kill the building power. They didn't know the security system wouldn't be affected, not that it matters since you can't see anything."

"The man that escaped was handcuffed in the secure waiting area beside the courtroom," the agent says. "Security found the cuffs hanging off the metal hook. The door has electronic security and must have failed with the building power."

"And they walked right out the front door," Gus says.

"The Second never intended to meet me. I was the fall guy the entire time. The jersey to stand out. The parking space right in the middle of the security camera's field of view. And the kicker, being seen outside Culver's office minutes before he's found dead."

"They made you," Gus says. "They knew who you were and used you."

"Seems like it." I turn to the Chief. "Who in your department called the media to tell them about the attorney? They had that information way too fast."

He shakes his head. "Wouldn't have happened without my clearance."

"They did it," Gus said. "The Second, or one of the other men. They needed you on the run. They needed the police to have a suspect so they could get away clean."

"What now, then?" SAC Hudson says.

CHAPTER 37

"Eddie?"

"Eva. It's so good to hear you. Are you home?"

"Yes. What the hell is going on? You're all over the news. Everyone from work is calling me."

"Any media outside the house?"

"No. Not that I can see."

"I need you to get out of there. Just grab your go bag from the closet and drive. Get up to Clem. He'll take care of you."

"Am I in danger?"

"I don't know. Maybe. I just need to make sure you're safe. Away from news trucks, people calling from work. Leave your phone at home. I'll contact Clem when it's clear."

"What's going on there? I can barely hear you," she says.

"It's about to get really loud," I say. "I love you."

"I can't wait for you to nuzzle my boobies again."

"He told you! Aww!" The side door of the state police helicopter slides shut. "Gotta go. Talk soon. Get to Clem's."

We lift off the ground and are moving forward before even clearing the buildings. Gus is beside me. We're both in full tactical gear along with six other agents from the San Antonio FBI SWAT team. A second helicopter is taking off behind us with SAC Hudson and another seven agents. Ninety minutes ago six trucks left with more than thirty agents and local SWAT. The second the warrant was handed to Gus, we were wheels up to meet the ground team at the compound.

"The Ruby compares themselves to Ruby Ridge and the Branch Davidians in philosophies, but claims to be peaceful," I say. We have headphones and mics turned to a private channel. "We can't let another Waco happen on our watch."

"Do you think it's possible? Are they arming themselves now to dig in?" Gus says.

I shake my head. "If I had to guess I'd say no. The Ruby doesn't seem like he's that invested in the whole martyr thing, but he also doesn't want to die. He built up the Sword to do his dirty work. They aren't trained killers. His followers at the ranch are not fighters. It's the Ruby's personal security that will shoot if given the chance. I counted eight of them, plus the Nepali."

"They armed?"

"I only saw them carry Desert Eagles," I say. "So, yes, but they are more likely to deafen you than actually hit you with a bullet."

"We have a BOLO out for the Sprinter van and photos of the men from the security tape circulating," Gus says. "At this point we have to risk being outed to the Ruby."

We go silent for the rest of the flight. We don't know if we are walking into a firefight or a mass surrender. Either way, we need to be prepared mentally. Gus and I have been side by side in the line of fire too many times to count and we're both still here to talk about it. I for one plan on tonight being another story to talk about over beers in a few weeks.

The radio chirps and the pilot tells us we are approaching the compound. The other helicopter is ahead of us. Search lights come on from both birds and scan the ground. There's no sign of anyone. The pickups are blocking the front gate.

"They might be barricaded in," I say.

Gus gives commands over the radio to the two helicopters full of agents. Orders are sent down to the ground teams as well.

The first chopper lands and agents are out both sides, their assault rifles raised as they dash to the buildings and trailers. We touch down beside the bonfire which still glows from being lit earlier in the evening.

"They were here recently and the trucks are inside the gate," I say.

The first cracks of gunfire come from the windows of the two houses. Agents respond quickly and accurately through the windows, then breach the door and finish the job. One man is killed, the other is taken alive with injuries.

More shots from the trailers. Agents won't shoot through walls. They must have eyes on targets, so defensive positions are taken and two canisters of tear gas are put through windows. The remaining men come out, hands over their faces.

"That was almost too easy," I say.

"I'll take easy," Gus says. "We don't get easy often enough."

"True. Let's head to the ranch."

We are back in the choppers and off the ground.

"Thirty seconds," Gus broadcasts.

The helicopters spread out from each other and go full speed. The six vans are already converging on the ranch, with that expected to be where the Ruby is, and perhaps the Nepali. Still no word of the Second and the other men from the Sprinter van.

"Ground team is ready," the pilot says.

"Tell them to go," Gus says.

The search lights under the helicopters light up the ranch grounds as agents come in from all four sides on foot, assault weapons raised and scanning in pattern to cover each other's asses without accidentally shooting one of their own men. They train regularly for these scenarios. Trigger and ammunition control is important to ensure everyone doesn't drain their magazines at once. Three round bursts to stop targets.

Still in the air, I see agents breach the farmhouse from front and back. The glow of the rifle-mounted lights come from the windows as they scan each room.

"Let's sit them down," I say.

The pilots bring the helicopters around and land away from each other on the wide open land between the main house and the barns. The rest of the agents unload first to join the sweep.

Alerts of "All clear" are coming through the headphones every few seconds as each building and room are gone through. Nobody is found.

SAC Hudson leads the teams at the barns. Gus and I head to the farmhouse. Agents are already coming out, weapons lowered in stand-down mode.

"Have you been inside?" Gus motions to the farmhouse.

"No. The only time I came to the ranch I walked around the grounds with the Ruby. We had breakfast on the front porch."

"How romantic."

We go room to room. We aren't sweeping, but are still alert, hands on our pistols. The house is bare inside, and not from having been cleared out quickly. There were simply no substantial furnishings. Folding chairs and camp chairs make up the brunt of the decorating, along with empty liquor bottles. Most rooms have old cot mattresses on the floor.

Upstairs we move to what would be the master bedroom. There's a twin bed on a box spring and no frame.

"Sure looks like the bedroom of the man who possesses the meaning of life," I say.

"Maybe the meaning of life is to not own anything."

"It could be."

We're back outside and stand looking from the side porch down past the helicopters to the barns.

"Hmm."

"What's up?" Gus says.

"When I was here there were women carrying stuff to the big barn from the house and the other buildings in white plastic corrugated boxes."

"Like the post office uses," Gus says.

"Exactly what I thought when I saw them. There weren't any inside, though."

Gus clicks his radio on. "Does anybody have eyes on white plastic boxes about two foot long by eighteen inches wide?"

It only takes a second for a response. "Sir, we have dozens of them in the barn. All empty."

Gus looks at me. "What are you thinking?"

"I'm thinking we pack up and get out of here."

CHAPTER 38

The agents clear out of the buildings and head back to the trucks which have pulled into the ranch. The two helicopters wind back up as Gus and I make our way to the one we rode in on.

"You sure about this?" Gus says. "We didn't find anything here."

"I'm sure."

The rotors get up to speed and the choppers lift off the ground. Their spotlights come on, swiveling around and lighting up the barns and the house as they elevate then turn and disappear into the night sky.

Gus and I are lying on our bellies on the ground under where our chopper had been sitting.

"Well that's a first," I whisper.

"Can't say I've ever done that either, or want to again."

Our black tactical gear blends in with the grass in the darkness and we stay still. It's hot as usual and we both have black balaclavas over our faces. Then we wait.

The first fifteen minutes of being still is tough. The next forty-five are worse. I feel ants crawling up inside my pants and I want to take a hot bath that lasts three days.

Gus's hand taps mine. I look down the hill.

The large barn door slides open about a foot then stops.

"Bingo," I whisper.

Everything is still again. A few minutes later it slides open farther.

Three large men in all black come out slowly, their movements giving away their training. Ex-military most likely, then government authorized mercenaries. And now, whatever this is. They have their Desert Eagles still in holsters and each have AR-15s raised. As the first three continue to move, the other five emerge from the door. Rifles scan. There's light on inside the barn and they are stepping into darkness, so their vision is compromised, but won't be for much longer.

I whisper as softly as I can. "We need to see the Ruby first."

Finally, at the back of the line of people exiting the barn, comes the Ruby.

"You good?" Gus whispers.

"Yup."

Gus clicks his radio and quickly gives the go order before the men with guns can react to the electronic chirp in the still night air.

"Go! Go! Go!"

Two dozen agents appear from as many directions, weapons raised and yelling commands. The men dressed in black start to fire at them and are quickly eliminated by the highly trained agents. Though likely good shots, they were outflanked and outplayed by FBI SWAT. Two of them drop their rifles and raise their hands in the air, preferring capture over dying for nothing more than a paycheck.

Gus and I are on our feet and running down the small hill, pistols raised, and get to the Ruby as he is being apprehended. All of the men are now face down on the ground with zip ties being placed on their wrists and ankles as searches for any more weapons on their bodies are conducted. The Desert Eagles are all confiscated and unloaded.

"Where are the followers?" I say.

Gus looks around with me.

"Gus, Eddie, you'll want to see this." SAC Hudson calls us over.

We follow him into the barn. A two-yard square door is raised from the opening in the floor. A full staircase leads underground. The door had been large enough it wasn't obvious, and was covered partially by rugs. The area underground is lit up and agents are moving around down there.

"Is it clear?" Gus says.

Hudson nods.

I follow Gus down the ladder. The area is as big as the dimensions of the barn above with a seven foot ceiling. Walls are lined with wood shelving holding enough food and provisions in the white plastic bins to wait out a nuclear holocaust. In one corner is a large desk with multiple monitors showing the feed from dozens of cameras across the ranch and at the compound four miles away. I scan the feeds and point.

"That was where I was sleeping," I say. "They were onto me. At least since the hooker."

"The what?" Gus says.

"I'll tell you later."

"Yes. Yes, you will."

There are voices and shuffling feet and we turn around. More than two dozen men and women are being brought out of a room with a solid metal door that had been locked from the outside. After they reach the top of the ladder they are zip tied and lined up with the rest to be sorted out later.

We step into the room. Lining the walls are folding tables covered with plastic-wrapped white cubes.

"Here's the drug operation," I say.

"So they are all complicit," Gus says.

"We'll have to see. Could be only a few of them. Some may not even have known this was here until they got locked up in here."

I go back to the camera feeds.

"What are you looking for?" Gus says.

"Him."

"The Nepali? You think he even shows up on camera?"

I chuckle. "True. He's probably vibrates at the perfect velocity to not be seen."

"He's not here, Eddie."

"Not that we can see. Maybe he stayed back in San Antonio or went a different direction after killing the ADA and the officer. Or he's watching everything we're doing."

"He knew who you were the whole time," Gus says. "Do you think he ID'd you to the Ruby or the Ruby already knew?"

"Does it matter?"

"True."

Hudson comes back to us. "We sent digital fingerprints to D.C. for immediate analysis. Thought you'd like to know his real name."

I take Hudson's phone. On the screen is a photograph of the Ruby. He is younger and skinnier.

"Well I'll be," I say. "His name is actually Donald Ruby. I guess he wasn't lying when he said he was from a long line of Rubies."

"He was a teacher in Ohio," Gus says. "High school social studies and history."

"I can actually see that," I say. "He has that teacher vibe."

Gus looks over at the Ruby, now face down on the ground, hands and feet zip tied. "So, what all are we booking him with?"

"Good question," I say. "There's the drugs, of course. We need to make sure we can tie him to the mission in San Antonio today and the murder of ADA Culver and the cop. Maybe the Second will turn on him when we catch him. He was never a true believer. Then trace all these guns. See what's legal, if any, and how they were acquired. There's possession of an EMP device. We have the death of Buster Ballard."

"He'd be an accomplice at best to Ballard."

"But we know, at least," I say. "We may be able to get Leocadia Ortiz's husband to flip on him to reduce his prison sentence. We find the rest of the men from the compound, some of them will go on record that they were forced to fight by the Ruby. Don't know if any will give up the Nepali. They're scared of him."

"What about you?" Gus says. "You scared of him?"

"Shitless."

"Think he'll show up again?"

"I don't think he's a revenge kind of guy, but he's been hitched to the Ruby for a while and I've gotten in his way twice now."

We watch the men and women being loaded into more vans that have arrived on scene.

"Most of them will be cut loose after giving their statements," Gus says. "If they didn't raise their guns and tell us everything we need to know. The few who did shoot didn't last long enough to make it off the ranch alive."

"It's a shame," I say. "These people were peaceful. They wanted only to live quietly, simply. The Ruby probably forced them to take the rifles to protect him, and they would have done anything for him."

"What do you think will happen to them?" Gus says.

"I think they'll keep trying to find their way. Maybe another Ruby will rise from their ranks, or a leader of some kind. Maybe not."

My gaze is out over the open plains obscured by darkness. We likely avoided another Ruby Ridge or Waco but something doesn't feel complete. I turn to Gus.

"I wanna drive back alone."

He looks at me then off into the nothingness I was staring at.

"You sure? It's a long drive."

"I'm sure. Need to pick up my gun and cellphone that are stashed down the road anyway."

He nods. "Figure those SUVs need to make it back to evidence."

I glance over at the two black Cadillacs and the ruby red Range Rover. "The red is a little flashy for me, but I'll take one of the black ones."

"Be safe."

"Where's the fun in that?"

CHAPTER 39

After nearly two weeks sleeping and living in filth, not showering, and never once feeling the cool air of an air conditioner, I have the AC set as low as it will go and the windows open in the Escalade because I can't stand my own smell. Even when I changed to fresh clothes and tactical gear before the raid, I didn't have time for a shower.

The road is empty once I clear the ranch. The glow of portable lighting the FBI set up is barely visible when I pull off the road a few miles away to retrieve the Glock 19 and satellite phone. At least I can call Eva while driving.

Back on the road I have cruise control set at a few miles over the posted limit. My eyes scan the dark horizon out of instinct.

There are days I miss working full time as an agent at the FBI. And other days I'm happy taking photographs of cheating husbands and idiots scamming their companies for workman's comp. It isn't great money, but it's easy. I don't go to bed at night feeling fulfilled, but I have Eva beside me and that's all that matters. I can take cases when I want to and breaks when I don't, though that doesn't happen often.

I owe Eva one of those breaks. A long one on a beach somewhere, preferably where the drinks are strong and the native language is not English. I need to do everything I can to keep her happy. Some day she'll get tired of being with a guy who comes home with a new scar every few months.

Movement in the rearview mirror and I glance at it. Only darkness. Just a light reflected off a street sign probably.

Is Spain nice this time of year? The south of France? I need to make sure my passport is up to date and tell Eva to take a few weeks off work.

Headlights come on and blind me in the reflections from my mirrors. The vehicle is only a few feet off the back of my SUV.

I tap the brakes to turn cruise control off and let the large vehicle slow down on its own. I watch to see if the other car passes me. It doesn't.

Instead I hear an engine rev higher and the back of the Escalade moves left with the impact. I'm lucky airbags don't go off or I'd be blind for a few seconds, or longer if anything flew into my eyes.

I have few doubts who is behind me, even though this technique doesn't feel like him. But it's either stop me here or wait until I'm back in a populated area to sneak up on me like he does. My guess is he wants to end it now. So do I.

The engine behind me revs again but instead of hitting

me, the lights move to the oncoming lane and the vehicle speeds up beside me. Once it matches speed I look over and see the black hoodie and the reflection of lights off the Nepali's dead eyes.

Still looking at each other, I slam on the brakes then crank the wheel left in a calculated risk at near seventy miles per hour. The front of the Escalade strikes the back half of the large Ford pickup the Nepali is driving and sends it into a spin in front me. As the front tires catch the dirt on the side of the road, the truck rolls. Meanwhile, the Escalade has been badly injured. The front left is lower after the impact, likely the front suspension is shattered. Still with forward momentum, my stopping power is greatly reduced. When I hit the brakes, the Cadillac disagrees with my decision but I eventually slow to a stop at least fifty yards from where the Nepali spun and rolled off the road.

I sit for a moment to make sure I'm still alive then check all my body parts for blood or impaled objects. All good. I'm still in pain from rolling out of the Corolla earlier today, but I count on the adrenaline rush to get me through the next few minutes.

Out of the Cadillac, I check the Glock and move toward the Ford pickup. It is laying on its roof about twenty feet off the road. I move down beside it, keeping my distance. Even in the dark I can tell nobody is inside the cab.

I spin, checking my six and farther, knowing he is here somewhere. If he was able to get out of the truck that fast, he is still able to strike. I want smooth ground beneath me and continue scanning, gun raised, until I'm in the middle of the blacktop.

It's dark. The headlights on the Ford truck the Nepali was in are smashed, and the Escalade is facing the other way up the road. I stop and listen. Nothing. Barely any animal sounds from the plains, the sounds I've grown so used to hearing the last week or so. I steady my breath. I now know the sounds that should be here and those that shouldn't.

I think back to the alley nearly a year ago where the Nepali ran past me so quickly, so effortlessly, the curved blade he is a master at using slicing my side. I didn't know I'd been cut until the next morning after almost bleeding out in bed beside Eva.

I keep my ears tuned to hear a footstep or scrape on the road. Holding my own breath, I hear something. Breathing. Strained. Hurt from the truck rolling, I can only hope.

"Hello, Eddie."

The voice comes from behind me and I spin. During my motion I see a black blur in the dark come at me. A fist strikes the inside of my right hand then comes back against my face as the barrel of the Glock is grabbed and thrown in one fluid motion.

My hands want to go to my body, to feel for warm blood coming out of a clean wound, but I need my hands up, ready. He got the jump on me again, but I can't let him keep his momentum.

I turn to look for him, for the black hood obscuring his face. As I move right he's there, coming at me again. I can see both hands and no blade. A fair fight, for now, if you can call it fair.

He comes with a right leg to my left knee then a spin to strike my head with a back fist. I see the kick just in time to shift weight away from it and turn with him in a movement that could look choreographed, two bodies in motion, inches from each other as arms and legs carry weight faster like a pendulum.

His fist glances off my head doing no damage. I change direction and come back around with a knee that lands firm in his gut. Not even a grunt or a sign of being hit comes from him.

Punches are exchanged. A series of lefts and rights from both of us, landing and blocking and attempted grapples to take control of the other, but all offenses are met with perfect defenses until we both step back at the same time to regroup.

There is a moment for a fighter when the fight changes. The fighter changes. It isn't anything physical that can be seen or studied, but a feeling, a state of being. Water and steam are both made of the same elements. Two hydrogen atoms and one oxygen. They are scientifically identical but completely different in how they appear, how they move. One fluid, the other vapor. A fighter goes from one state to another while being the same person. From water to steam. Our physical restraints are still there, but the reaction time between synapses firing is decreased.

We engage again. A furious but exact series of strikes. No one punch or kick is designed to end the fight or knock the other out, but to weaken the opponent until advantage is gained.

He is using a combination of multiple disciplines, going from style to style seamlessly as if it were one art form. He knows more than I do. He's better than I am. It is becoming a game of attrition. I only need to last long enough to tire him out and make a move.

I lunge in with a left punch with no real intent behind it. Just as he leans back to avoid it, an acrid smell fills the air followed by a hissing sound that grows in volume quickly. I drop to the ground just as the Ford pickup ignites into flames thirty feet from us. The explosion follows a few moments later, leaving the burning carcass of the mangled truck behind. Small bits of shrapnel strike me and I can tell by the way the Nepali is moving, he's been hit too.

Back on my feet I stay in motion, circling him and striking when my back is to the flames, my form obscured in silhouette. Quick straight punches that come out of nowhere. He sees my ploy and works to keep the fire beside us.

The night sky brightens as the sound of the flames are muted from above. One of the helicopters hovers, its searchlight creating a circle on the road, our ring, our octagon, our colosseum. The black FBI vehicles pull up and headlights further illuminate us as we fight.

Neither of us is slowing down, but he's been faster than me since the beginning. I pace myself and rely on accuracy over acceleration, deflection instead of defense. Let his body move him farther with each punch and kick, to send himself off mark where I can land a blow to the side of his head, his ribs.

There is no real advantage with the flames to my back now, but I turn to use it one more time. He expects it and lands a ferocious kick that sends me backwards off the road, tripping on scrub and landing near the fire. He's back on top of me before I am even upright again, but I use my motion to land an uppercut to his ribs followed by an elbow on his face. For the first time I see a stumble from him, a moment of fatigue, and I don't rest though I feel I may collapse.

A kick to his gut that pulls back and elevates to bring my shin to his nose. I feel cartilage give and even in the red glow of the flames I can see the blood ooze from his nostrils.

He comes with an attack, slower than he's been, and I easily block most of the punches and turn to minimize the kicks. It ends in a hold, our faces aimed at each other while I have his left arm in a lock. For the first time from the Nepali, I see a beaten man, and a beaten man can be more dangerous than one that is winning. I keep the lock on his elbow and rotate my hips as I drop down to a knee and feel his shoulder disengage from its socket. Even with that comes no cry of pain from him.

I stand and step away. He's on his knees beside the roaring fire, the burning paint and melting plastic scents lining my nose.

"Let's end this," I say. "You're under arrest for the murder of Bernard Culver."

He looks up at me. And he smiles.

With a sudden movement he is rushing at me. His right arm comes from behind his back with the curved blade extended and swinging toward me, back and forth, as he stumbles to reach me. I watch the movement, time my actions, and as the blade passes across his body I rotate and move along with him, my hands going to his holding the blade. It is slow motion from there. Without even pausing, I keep my momentum and feel his wrist snap as I bend against the joint and remove the hilt of the blade from his grip. In a tight rotation I come around to face him. My right hand, now with the curved knife, swings. I don't even feel the edge cut through his skin, but know it did.

The Nepali stops moving and stands still, his back to the flames, as a river of blood appears from a perfectly straight line across his abdomen. I had gone deeper than I even realized.

He looks down at the blood then up at me. When a warrior is killed, they only hope it is to someone worthy. An adversary that deserved the victory, not a bullet from a hundred yards away. Another fighter. Another warrior. For someone like the Nepali, that is the only honorable death.

His eyes meet mine and I see him accept his fate, his death, and the slightest of nods. I return the nod.

The Nepali struggles to move his feet, but does, small steps back away from me. Not in fear of being struck again. The fight is over. We both know it.

The flames kick up behind him, drawn to the mass coming into it. He takes a longer stride back as the fire begins to wrap around him. The defeated body finally falls backwards, fully into the dancing orange and red life form that is taking him.

Gus comes up beside me and watches the decaying ruins of a warrior.

I turn to him. He looks at me.

"Why the hell didn't you shoot him?" I say.

"I didn't think you'd want me to."

CHAPTER 40

Gus threatens to fly me back to the hospital at Salt Creek. I tell him they'll never get all the Silverados out of the parking lot in time for us to land, so we head back toward Austin. A medic on scene checks me out and finds nothing serious, just a lot of bruises and scrapes and small pieces of melted pickup truck embedded in my skin.

I want to call Eva but it is too loud in the chopper. Gus texts Clem to let them know we are headed back and give the mostly all clear.

Gus motions and I turn to a private channel on the headphones.

"That was a helluva thing," he says.

I nod and it hurts. "It sure was."

"I got something for you."

"You shouldn't have."

Gus picks up a black nylon bag and carefully pulls out the Nepali's curved blade wrapped in plastic. "It needs to go through evidence, but I figure since there won't be a trial, it can go on permanent loan to you, if you want it."

"He was a great warrior," I say. "It's almost a shame he's dead. You did confirm he's dead, right?"

"We can safely say he's well done."

I fall asleep for the remainder of the flight and only wake when the skids of the helicopter touch down just outside Austin Memorial Hospital. A team is beside the landing pad with a stretcher. I'm helped out, more sore than anything, and lay down as I'm strapped for the ride back up into the hospital. I look around the faces and finally see hers on my left.

"Hey, beautiful."

"Hey, yourself," Eva says.

"I love you."

"I love you, too, asshole."

"I deserve that."

"Yes, you do." She smiles and fades away as I'm rolled into an exam area and the curtain is pulled shut.

I have an I.V. in my left arm for fluids and ask if I can be given something to rest. The nurses check and a drug is injected into the port on the line.

There are moments when you know things have to change. That you can't go on like you have been. It isn't good for you or for those you love. It isn't fair to Eva or even Gus. I barely see my sister and her family anymore.

This is one of those moments as I lay on a bed having pieces of metal roughly extracted my body by some nurses taking out Eva's revenge on me for putting her through hell time and time again.

But, as soon as those moments come, you know they will pass. It is hard, if not impossible, for someone to change so quickly, so radically, from who they are. I faced down a warrior tonight. A formidable opponent I've faced before. I was victorious this time and he's gone. But fighters keep fighting.

I know who I am and what I do. I'm good at it. I've been good at it for a long time, and maybe a long time is long enough. It's easy to say I'm done. No more cases. No more chasing people. No more getting shot at and stabbed. Well, it sounds easy to say, but isn't when it's all you know. But I'm saying it, for now at least.

The one thing I know I need in this world is somewhere beyond the pale blue curtain surrounding me. She has changed my life for the better, put up with more than any person should, and comforted me when I needed it. I don't want there ever to be a day I don't go home to Eva. Running a bar and music parlor in Austin is a lot less dangerous than working for the FBI or being a private detective. So I think I'll give that a try for a while.

I fall asleep from the drugs. There are no dreams that I remember.

I wake twelve hours later with a combination of feeling refreshed and that sleeping medicine hangover. Water helps. Gus arrives looking no less fresh than he had when we got to the hospital.

"What's up?" I say. "You don't look like you slept at all."

"I didn't."

He pulls the curtain closed and drags a rolling stool over and sits beside my bed.

"Just got back from San Antonio," he says. "Border patrol found the van in Brownsville. We think some of the men walked across into Matamoros."

"Just some of them?"

"State police have the Second, real name, and I shit you not, Henry Higgins."

"Seriously?" I laugh. "I should have asked him if the rain in Spain falls mainly on the plain. Do we know if he's talking?"

"We have people in the room. He's giving everything he has on Ruby. I figure he'll be in federal custody any time now until an official deal is negotiated. He won't walk free, but will likely get a reduced sentence."

"Guess this is wrapping up nicely. The rest of the guys will be harder to find since we don't have names for them."

"That's the funny thing," Gus says. "We do. The Second, sorry, Higgins, kept their driver's licenses and anything else they had. We know who all of them are."

"Will certainly help border patrol spot them."

"And we found this." Gus hands me the typical Office Depot grade filing folder we call jackets. There's three pieces of paper in it.

I read through the pages then do it again in case I missed anything. When done, I hand them back and lean back, looking up at the grid of ceiling tiles. He was the one man I never did know, but who started all of this.

"Any chance you'd—" Gus didn't let me finish the sentence.

"I already pulled some strings and have us two seats on a state police plane. They said it was the least they can do since we wrapped this whole thing up for them."

CHAPTER 41

After landing in Yuma, Arizona, the plane stops near the private hangers. Gus and I climb down the stairs into the heat, both of us wearing suits and ties. The large black Ford pickup is idling nearby and our new detective friend Raf climbs out. He's wearing a sports coat with a bolo tie and a cowboy hat that looks like it only comes out for special occasions.

"Thanks for meeting us, Raf," Gus says.

"*De nada, mi amigos.* Don't mention it."

The inside of the truck is probably the coldest it has ever been but I'm not about to ask him to make it warmer, especially with a suit on. The drive through the city doesn't take long. We pull up in front of a two-story stucco home on a street full of the same style house, all slightly different. It's a nice neighborhood. Not what we'd expected. A BMW SUV and an Audi sedan are in the driveway.

The three papers in the jacket Gus had handed to me in the hospital were a picture of Buster Ballard's driver's license, a copy of his GED for finishing the requirements for a high school diploma, and a single page rap sheet of crimes he'd committed. There was only one listed. At age seventeen he had been arrested trying to steal a six pack of beer in his school backpack from a convenience store. The store's owner had a reputation for pressing charges, and did so with Buster. That was it. He was not a career criminal and had never spent time in a jail cell.

The curtain beside the front door is pulled to the side before we even ring the bell, and the door opens.

"Can I help you?" She's maybe sixty-years-old and dressed well for what appears to be a normal Saturday morning at home.

"Yes, ma'am. I'm Detective Rafael Morales with the Yuma Police Department. These are Special Agents Gus Ramirez and Eddie Holland with the FBI."

The woman's face drains of color and I worry she'll fall down.

"Are you Emmy Ballard?" Gus says.

She nods.

"May we come in?" I say.

Still looking stunned as if she already knows what is coming, she takes a step back and we enter her house.

"Is your husband home?" Gus says.

A slight nod and she steps to the end of the hall. "Ben, can you come here. We have some men who want to talk to us."

"Shall we sit?" I say?

Another slight nod and she motions to the sofas and chairs in the first room. It looks like one of those rooms that nobody is supposed to enter or use, everything perfectly placed and clean.

Her husband comes in as we're about to sit and introductions happen again. Emmy Ballard has barely sat down across from us when she speaks.

"This is about Buster." It wasn't a question.

We all nod then realize we are all nodding and try to not look like a bunch of idiots nodding. I look at Gus to let him continue.

The story is told as best as we know it, starting from when the tip line phone call came in and filling in whatever we could. Details about the San Antonio activities are kept slim, partly because Buster was not a part of them, and because the couple had seen the coverage on the news.

"So, our Buster was a part of this . . . this . . . what even is it? A gang? A cult?"

"He was. It appears he met up with them here in Yuma when they were camped out at the old airfield, then moved to Texas with them."

"And he died in a fight? What kind of fight?"

"The group had a rite of passage, if you will. The final one being a series of fights. At first against some of the other men, then against another man, an experienced fighter."

"Buster was always very good at Tae-Kwon-Do," Ben Ballard says. "He won so many trophies and tournaments. He was very good. But he died in a fight?"

"Yes, sir."

"This man who killed him, what is his name?"

Gus shakes his head. "We don't know. He was someone we had dealings with before, but have never known his name. He goes only by the Nepali. It's thought that he was a warrior and an assassin in the Nepali military."

There is no look of shock or disgust on the parents face. Not even disbelief. We could just as easily be telling them the premise of *Dancing With the Stars*. They're in shock and will take time to process.

"The Nepali," Emmy Ballard says. "Where is he now?"

Gus looks over at me. I make eye contact with her.

"I killed him, Mrs. Ballard. He's dead."

Buster Ballard's mother looked me in the eyes and I held her unblinking gaze for what seemed an eternity before she finally spoke again.

"Good."

CHAPTER 42

I get out of the large bed naked. Eva is relaxed from our shared display of love and gratitude toward each other that just occurred. There's a cart with the remains of breakfast still beside the door and I pluck a grape off the stem and pop it in my mouth.

"Mmm. Juicy."

We haven't left the hotel room in three days. I walk to the curtains and pull them open to show the long beach of Nice, France, below. We are on top the cliff at the end where it curves, our own private balcony extending even farther out.

The rain hasn't stopped since before we landed. The weather reports say it is the longest streak of wet weather they've experienced in high season in a hundred years.

"Sorry about the rain, sweetie," I say.

"It's raining? I hadn't noticed," Eva says.

I go for another grape.

"Should I get dressed?" I say.

"Then you'll just have to get undressed again."

"That's a fair point."

I get back in bed beside her and she curls up to me. I can feel her still sweaty skin against mine.

"It's been quite a while and I want you to know I haven't forgotten about, well, you know."

"About proposing to me in a room full of retired Army Rangers?"

"Yeah. That."

"I've barely thought about it myself," she says.

"Really?"

"Knowing you want me is enough right now. Maybe tomorrow or maybe next year we'll know it's the right time. But for now I have you and you have me and the world is perfect."

We lay there in each other's warmth for a while.

"Things have been crazy, but I do have some big news for you," she says. "And no, I'm not pregnant."

"Whew, okay. Thanks for getting that out of the way quickly."

"The practice offered me a job."

"That's incredible." I roll her into me and squeeze her tight, kissing the top of her head.

"There's more. A partner is retiring and they actually want me to take his place. It's a big investment, but it can really set us up for the future. For our future."

"Our future," I say. "I like the sound of that. And you already told them yes, right?"

She rolls over on top of me and straddles my body, looking right down at me.

"I did."

"Then let's celebrate."

ABOUT THE AUTHOR

I spent my childhood moving from house to house in a small Arkansas town with my father and sister. There were no family pictures on the walls, only a few small framed school photos on flat surfaces.

Every possible space was covered with bookshelves.

My dad had collected since he was young and continued until the day he passed away in November of 2020. He always joked that his Doubleday Book Club membership number was 1.

He carried a book with him everywhere. In a town where it was not unnormal to see people carrying bibles, he had the latest fiction releases fresh from the presses and delivered to our door.

My sister and I were readers, not surprisingly. There were no limits on what we read. The terms middle grade fiction and young adult fiction weren't really a thing then. So, it was Stephen King well before I was old enough for it. I did occasionally find more age appropriate titles. I checked *Bridge to Terabithia* out from the school library. It wrecked me. It still wrecks me.

The Outsiders was formative for me, especially being in a small town not too far from Tusla, where S.E. Hinton wrote it as a teenager. She was and is an inspiration.

I always loved writing. I was the rare student who enjoyed the writing assignments in school, as long as they were fiction, of course. In college I wanted to take Freshman

Composition over and over, but they wouldn't let me. The teacher was a wanna-be-novelist who would read from his own works in progress in class.

I spent a short time in Northern California and renewed my love of John Steinbeck there, picking up copies of *Cannery Row, Sweet Thursday, The Pearl,* and everything else I could find at the Cupertino Public Library. I would drive somewhere Steinbeck himself had been and read. Yeah. Nerdy. I wrote some short stories during that time, including one I entered in a competition through the Steinbeck Center in Salinas, California. I did not win.

Years later, stories started coming through my head. I finally started writing stuff down. My first novel took me years because I couldn't accept that I was writing a book. At some point, though, after thirty thousand words or so, you come to grips with it. That book became my first release, *The South Coast,* the first in the Eddie Holland detective series.

Since then, I've released seven novels including one middle grade fiction so my son could read something I'd written. *Ruby Rising* is my eight novel and I recently completed what will be my ninth, another middle grade fiction.

I miss my dad everyday. He wasn't perfect. But who is? I read because of him and I write because of him. What more can you ask?

THANKS

Shea Megale is the type of friend everyone needs. Getting full of yourself? Shea will set you straight. Got writer's block? Shea will send you memes for days to help you avoid writing. Thank you for editing *Ruby Rising*. You are an incredible friend, editor and author. Please buy Shea's books *This is Not a Love Scene* and *American Boy* (as S.C. Megale).

Edward Hutchison, a great critic, proofreader, and friend. He is the author of the epic southern gothic autobiographical *Hard Winter*.

Laura Buchwald for being a wonderful friend and inspiration, as well as my cohost on our top rated, #1 reviewed podcast with over 30 million listeners worldwide (not all or any of that may be true), *People Who Do Things*, available on Apple Podcasts or wherever you listen to podcasts! We talk to each other about writing as well as chat with guests which keeps the creativity flowing in my brain. Watch for Laura's debut novel in 2024!

And thank you to the writers who have inspired me most:

S.E. Hinton
Barbara Kingsolver
Stephen King
Katherine Applegate
John Steinbeck
Robert B. Parker